THE TEXAS TATTLER

All the news that's barely fit to print!

Fortune Patriarch's "Secret" Nuptials on Hold

Despite a string of dead ends in the FBI investigation to recover his kidnapped grandson, Ryan Fortune, head of the Texas Fortune empire, has sworn that round-the-clock search efforts will continue. And if a national baby hunt isn't enough to keep a mogul up nights, his soon-to-be ex-wife, Sophia, is playing pinch-'n-spit in divorce negotiations—and holding out for the farm, or in the Fortunes' case, the whole dang *ranch*.

In the whirlwind of scandal, Ryan and Lily Redgrove have put off plans for their long-awaited wedding. Between shelling out a multimillion dollar ransom, an astronomical divorce settlement and enough cash for a Texas-sized engagement solitaire, will our very own "poor little rich boy" have more

than a few measly million left to pay for the wedding-to-end-all-weddings?

All the world's a-flutter with the shocking news of superstar sexpot Ciara Wilde's shocking disappearance—from her own Hollywood nuptials! *Tattler* roving reporters swear to a Ciara sighting at a remote cabin inhabited by dashing international TV newsman Jace Lockhart, Fortune in-law. Ciara may have resisted the casting couch, but can she keep from cozying up with Jace on the *cabin* couch...?

D1007753

About the Author

RUTH LANGAN

Award-winning and bestselling author Ruth Langan
creates characters that *Affaire de Coeur* magazine has called
"so incredibly human the reader will expect them to come
over for tea."

Over the years, Ruth has given more than thirty workshops
around the country to aspiring writers. She has given
dozens of print, radio and TV interviews, including *Good
Morning America* and CNN news, and has been quoted
in such diverse publications as *The Wall Street Journal,
Cosmopolitan* and *The Detroit Free Press*. A co-founder of
the Greater Detroit Chapter of Romance Writers of America
and a charter member of RWA, Ruth is also a member of the
Detroit Women Writers, Novelist, Inc. and Sisters in Crime.

These days finding time to write is not as difficult as it
was. In fact, Ruth and her husband jog several miles each
day to get her away from the word processor. But Ruth
knows, from the letters she receives, that the hours she
spends writing give her readers many more hours of happy
reading.

Watch for Ruth Langan's brand-new contemporary
miniseries from Silhouette books:
THE WILDES OF WYOMING, books 1-3
February 2000, April 2000, June 2000
Silhouette Intimate Moments

And watch for the debut of her new historical miniseries:
THE SIRENS OF THE SEA
late summer 2000
Harlequin Historicals

RUTH LANGAN

Snowbound
Cinderella

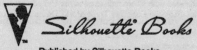

Silhouette Books

Published by Silhouette Books

America's Publisher of Contemporary Romance

Special thanks and acknowledgment are given to Ruth Langan for her contribution to The Fortunes of Texas series.

 SILHOUETTE BOOKS

ISBN 0-373-65035-3

SNOWBOUND CINDERELLA

Visit us at www.romance.net

Printed in U.S.A.

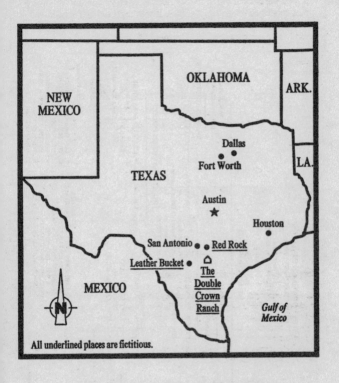

All underlined places are fictitious.

THE FORTUNES OF TEXAS

KINGSTON FORTUNE (d)

1st marriage **PATIENCE TALBOT** (d)
- Teddy §

2nd marriage **SELENA HOBBS** (d)

MIRANDA
m Lloyd Carter (D)

KANE **GABRIELLE** ⑧

RYAN

1st marriage **JANINE LOCKHART** (d)

MATTHEW ⑫
m
Claudia Beaumont
- Bryan

DALLAS ④
m 1st marriage
Sara Andersen (d)
2nd marriage m
Maggie Perez

VANESSA ②***VICTORIA** ⑩
m
Devin Kincaid

ZANE

† ROSITA and RUBEN PEREZ

Anita Carmen Frieda **CRUZ** ③
m
Savanah Clark

MAGGIE ④
1st marriage
m
Craig Randall (D)

Travis

2nd marriage
m
Dallas Fortune

2nd marriage **SOPHIA BARNES**

CLINT LOCKHART
brother of
JACE LOCKHART ⑥

James a.k.a. Taylor

CAMERON (d)
m **MARY ELLEN LOCKHART**

HOLDEN ① **LOGAN** ⑤ **EDEN** ⑦
m
Lucinda Brightwater

Amanda Sawyer*
Sue*
m
Emily Applegate

LILY REDGROVE
m
Chester Cassidy (d)

COLE* ⑪ **HANNAH** ⑨ **MARIA**

KEY
- * Child of affair
- d Deceased
- D Divorced
- m Married
- *** Twins
- —— Affair
- † Loyal ranch staff
- § Kidnapped by maternal grandfather

TITLES:
1. MILLION DOLLAR MARRIAGE
2. THE BABY PURSUIT
3. EXPECTING...IN TEXAS
4. A WILLING WIFE
5. CORPORATE DADDY
6. SNOWBOUND CINDERELLA
7. THE SHEIKH'S SECRET SON
8. THE HEIRESS AND THE SHERIFF
9. LONE STAR WEDDING
10. IN THE ARMS OF A HERO
11. WEDLOCKED?!
12. HIRED BRIDE

THE FORTUNES OF TEXAS™

 Meet the Fortunes of Texas

Jace Lockhart: This veteran reporter was under doctor's orders to relax, but the sexy stranger trapped in the isolated cabin with him was sending his blood pressure sky-high. And soon, warm embraces became more than a means for survival.

Ciara Wilde: The gorgeous movie star wasn't used to men loving her for herself. She wanted a man who saw beneath her silver-screen persona—and she was determined to find out if her romance with Jace was more than a snowbound affair.

Matthew and Claudia Fortune: Wedded bliss turned to sorrow when their precious baby boy was kidnapped. Will the stress of waiting and wondering about the fate of their little Bryan take a toll on their marriage?

Eden Fortune: This single mom didn't plan to fall in love again, but that didn't mean her four-year-old son couldn't ask for a father....

For Nora, who keeps challenging me to fly
And for Tom, who never lets me fall

One

Jace Lockhart maneuvered the Jeep up the steep mountain road. Every once in a while he cracked the window and sucked in frigid air to stay alert. He'd been awake for more than twenty-four hours now. First the flight from Bosnia to Paris to New York. Then the long lines for Customs at La Guardia. Then another flight to El Paso, where he'd waited yet again to rent a vehicle.

He opened the window, filling his lungs. Then, for good measure, he fiddled with the radio until he found Springsteen and cranked it up a notch. The motion of the windshield wipers seemed just a little too hypnotic. He didn't need to fall asleep at the wheel. On top of that, the rain had turned to snow, and the winding roads were slick with ice, demanding complete concentration. He couldn't afford to take his mind off the treacherous route for even a second.

Not that he minded. Anything was better than the dark thoughts that had been crowding his mind for the past months. All he'd been able to think about was Ireina. The way she'd looked, in the instant when the bomb had struck. And the sound of her screams, echoing through his mind, as she'd been torn from his arms. And the shattered body he'd had to identify at the makeshift morgue.

Even in sleep there was no release. The sights, the sounds, the horror of it all stalked him nightly, leaving him dreading a return to his bed.

It had been Brad Thompson, the overseas director of news at the network, who had first broached the subject of a leave of absence. At first Jace had resisted, believing that hard work was the cure. He'd plunged himself into even more work than before. He accepted endless assignments that nobody else wanted to cover, in far-flung towns and villages in eastern Europe. He'd slept in run-down hostels and flea-bitten inns, chasing stories of hatred and bombing and terrorism, of neighbor attacking neighbor, village against village, until, eventually, he'd begun to think there was nothing good or decent left in the world. The news events he found himself covering had begun to seem like one big nightmare, playing over and over.

He'd eventually become convinced that what he needed was a complete change of scenery, if he was ever going to put the past behind him and get on with his life.

This offer seemed heaven-sent. When his sister, Mary Ellen, had suggested it, Jace had leapt at the chance. What he wanted, even more than to be surrounded by loving family, was solitude. Some time to heal the scars, both physically and emotionally. Then, and only then, would he be ready to be around people again.

He rubbed absently at his leg, as if to erase the

pain that had become his constant companion. The surgeon had said it should mend in time. But Jace suspected that the shadow of pain would linger for a lifetime. Like the scar that marred his right cheek. Like the memory of Ireina. Even the lightest touch, or the slightest thought, reminded him that both his scars and his memories were still tender. And if he probed too deeply, he'd expose a nerve.

He spotted the little country church by the side of the road. Lights from inside flooded through the stained-glass windows like a beacon in the storm. If the driving should become impossible, he decided, he'd return here and seek sanctuary.

He turned the wheel, swinging off the main road and onto a dirt lane that led to the cabin. The lane was overgrown with tall trees, their branches quickly becoming heavy with snow. The steeper the climb, the more treacherous the road became, until at last, after several twists and turns, it seemed impossible to go on. The car swerved and nearly went off the road before the tires gripped and the Jeep darted ahead, coming to a stop inches from the cabin.

Jace felt a sense of relief that he'd finally reached his destination. Another hour and even the main roads would be impassable.

He switched off the engine and sat a moment, staring at the darkened log cabin. It was little more than a blur against the curtain of falling snow. The original cabin had been one large room, with a small galley kitchen and a loft that served as a bedroom. That would have been more than enough for his needs. But in recent years a master suite had been added, with a king-size bed and walk-in closet, as well as a bathroom containing both a shower and a hot tub. He intended to put it all to good use, especially the hot tub. It might be exactly what his injuries required to heal. If not, at least he would have the healing power of solitude.

With a sigh he forced himself into action, catching up his duffel bag and tossing the strap of his carryall over his shoulder before stepping out into the snowdrifts. He tramped up the wide wooden steps, grateful that the porch running the length of the cabin shielded him from the swirling snow—snow laced with ice that was beginning to sting like shrapnel. This simple spring storm had quickly become a full-blown blizzard.

He juggled the duffel and carryall while he fumbled with the key. When he'd managed to open the door, he stepped into the darkness and nudged the door shut with his hip.

"You move a muscle and you're dead." The woman's voice sounded a little too breathy. But whether from fear or anger, Jace couldn't determine. He froze as he felt the muzzle of the rifle jammed against his ribs. In the same instant, a blinding beam from a flashlight flooded his eyes.

His voice was low with fury. "Who the hell are you?"

"I'll ask the questions, buster. And you'd better have some very good answers, or you'll answer to this rifle."

She took a step closer, and as his eyes adjusted to the light, he realized she was a wild-eyed, gorgeous blonde, wearing nothing more than sexy underwear. "Now who are you, and what are you doing here in the middle of nowhere?"

His words were tight, angry. "My name is Jace Lockhart. My sister Mary Ellen Fortune owns this cabin."

His answer was greeted with stunned silence.

Jace took no more than a moment to figure the odds before he swung his duffel bag, knocking the rifle from the woman's hands. As it clattered to the floor he tossed aside his carryall and in one quick motion wrapped his arms around her, pinning her arms to her sides. The flashlight dropped from her fingers and the light flickered for a moment, then the cabin was plunged into darkness.

His voice was a rasp of fury against her temple. "Now *I'll* ask the questions. And I'd better like your answers. Who the hell are you?"

"My name is...Ciara."

The way she hesitated, he figured she was probably making this up as she went along. "Okay, Ciara, or whatever your name is. What are you doing in my family cabin?"

"I'm..." Her voice faltered and she had to swallow several times before she found the courage to speak. "I'm a friend of Eden Fortune."

"Eden? My niece?"

"Yes. She told me the cabin would be empty. Isolated and...private. She never said a word about you."

His tone grew thoughtful. "She wouldn't have known. Until now, I've been out of the country. And I swore my sister to secrecy about my return."

Jace felt heat building inside him, and blamed it on the rifle. Having the business end of a gun pointed at the heart tended to make a man sweat. Still, it didn't help to have a living, breathing, half-naked Barbie doll pressing against him. It had been the better part of a year since he'd held a woman, but his body, it seemed, hadn't forgotten the proper responses.

He released her and in one fluid movement bent and retrieved the rifle and flashlight. When he switched on the beam he saw the way her eyes widened, and could read the fear in them.

"Don't worry. I'm not going to shoot you. Unless you decide to come at me with another weapon. Then you'll just have to accept the consequences."

"I don't want any trouble." She lifted a hand to shield her eyes. "I thought...I thought you were here because you'd found out that I was hidi—that I was here." She cursed herself for her lapse. But he seemed too angry to notice.

"Then you can relax. The only reason I'm here is to be alone." He slowly circled the room with the light until he located a lamp on a nearby end table. He stepped over his luggage and switched it on, flooding the cabin with lamplight.

Now he could see the rugged, oversize furniture

grouped around a magnificent stone fireplace that soared all the way to the high-beamed ceiling.

"That's better." He turned in time to see the young woman glance down at herself with dismay. When she looked up, he was boldly staring. He didn't bother to look away.

She had a fantastic body, displayed in the most provocative manner possible. He looked her down, then up, from those long, long legs, to the lavender lace thong. His throat went dry and he forced his gaze upward. Her waist was so small he was certain his hands could easily span it. The bra was nothing more than two tiny bits of lavender lace, revealing more than they covered. And what they revealed was a body that would make any man's pulse go haywire. Then there was the face. Lovely enough to grace magazine covers. Full, pouty lips, at the moment turned down into a frown. High cheekbones that a model would kill for. A small perfect nose, and arched brows over eyes that were more green than blue. Her hair was a riot of soft blond waves that fell to her shoulders.

For one wild moment he wondered whether he was imagining this whole thing. This woman was too beautiful to be real. And this whole situation had the feeling of some fantasy gone awry. Maybe he really was losing it, and his imagination had taken over his senses.

To her credit she didn't flinch or try to cover herself. With her hands on her hips she returned the stare. "Seen enough?" The words came from between clenched teeth. Had she been a cat, he thought, she'd have been hissing and spitting.

"You didn't leave much for the imagination." He nearly grinned before he caught himself. "But you might want to put on some clothes before you catch a chill."

She turned away and stormed into the bedroom. Over her shoulder she called, "While I'm doing that, you can return your luggage to your car. Since I was here first, you'll just have to leave and find yourself a lodge somewhere nearby."

He walked to the window and stared morosely at the snowdrifts that were already up to the porch. "Sorry I can't oblige you. I'm afraid we're stuck with each other. At least for tonight."

She came running, tying the sash of her robe as she did. Her frown was more pronounced. "What do you mean?"

"See for yourself." He pointed. "Looks like we're in the middle of a spring blizzard. Nobody's going anywhere until it blows over."

Like a child, she pressed her face to the window and peered out into the darkness. What she saw had her closing her eyes against the spurt of anger and frustration. Then, unwilling to believe what she'd seen, she walked to the front door and yanked it open. Snow blew in on a rush of bitter wind, nearly snatching the door from her grasp.

Ciara sighed with disgust. The last thing she wanted was to share this cabin for even one night with this stranger. With anyone. She wanted—needed desperately—to be alone.

With a shiver she leaned into the door, forcing it closed. For several seconds she stayed where she was, her forehead against the door, listening to the howling wind outside. Then, taking a deep breath she turned and crossed the room, determined to make the best of this intolerable situation.

"I'm sorry about—I don't think I could have shot you."

"Now there's a comforting thought."

She flushed. "I just thought I'd be alone up here."

"Yeah. Me too." Jace shrugged out of his jacket and tossed it carelessly over the back of the sofa. Then he crossed to the fireplace, piled several logs on the grate and added kindling, watching until a thin flame began licking along the bark. Next he rummaged through his duffel until he located the sack of groceries. "I'm going to make some coffee. Want some?"

"Thanks." He moved so quickly that she found herself trapped between him and the counter in the kitchen area.

He felt the press of her body, but he didn't show it. He kept his gaze deliberately averted. But in his mind's eye he could still see the way she'd looked without the robe. It wasn't something a man could easily forget.

"How long have you been here?" He measured coffee into the filter, then poured water and plugged in the coffeemaker.

"Since this morning." Ciara brushed past him, annoyed by the little rush of heat as her body skimmed his. It was a body that was difficult to ignore. He had the taut, firm look of an athlete, with muscled arms and shoulders straining the sleeves of a charcoal sweater. She was a tall woman, yet he was taller easily by a head. Well over six feet. Thick auburn hair, with touches of gray at the temples, was badly in need of a trim. It fell in disarray over his collar.

Still tingling from the contact, she put as much distance as possible between them, settling herself on the sofa in front of the fire. "I got here before noon."

"I didn't see a car." He searched through the cupboards until he located two mugs.

"Eden told me there was a small shed in back. I parked there."

He nodded. "Something new, I guess. But then, I haven't been here in years."

"Where've you been?"

"Out of the country. Do you take cream or sugar?"

"Just a pinch of sugar." She watched as he moved efficiently around the kitchen, stashing eggs in the refrigerator, bread in the bread bin. He was obviously a man accustomed to being on his own and taking care of his own needs.

He filled two mugs with steaming coffee and carried them to the sofa. He handed one to her before settling himself beside her and stretching out his long legs toward the warmth of the fire. Until now, he hadn't known how cold he was. Or how utterly weary. The long hours of traveling were beginning to take their toll.

She sipped. Sighed. "Umm. This coffee is fantastic."

He tasted, then nodded his agreement. "I found it at a little store not far from the airport. I couldn't believe they'd have fresh-ground coffee at such a place."

"I guess you have been out of the country awhile." She chuckled. "Everybody, including gas stations, is selling designer coffee." She glanced over. "Where exactly have you been?"

"Here and there." He shrugged, frowned, obviously annoyed by the question. "Where's your home?"

It was apparent that he was a man who didn't like to talk about himself. All right, Ciara thought. She'd play it his way, though most of the men she knew in her line of work loved nothing better than to go on and on about themselves and their accomplishments. "I live in California."

"What part?"

Her voice unexpectedly lowered at the thought of the horrible scene she'd fled. Her impending wedding in two weeks to film star Brendan Swift had turned into a media circus. There had been a television crew on her doorstep. Another parked at the end of her drive. They'd trailed her for miles before she managed to lose them. "Malibu."

The anger in her tone had him looking over at her.

"You don't care for it? I've always thought it was pretty country."

"It can be pretty. I like the ocean. I just don't always like—the storms. They can get downright mean."

He had the idea she wasn't talking about the weather. He stared down into his cup and felt the quick slice of pain as he remembered. "I know a little about storms."

She was watching the fire, unaware that her voice took on an even harder edge. "I've ridden out a few of my own. But lately, I find myself sick of them."

"Yeah. Well..." He drained his cup, stood. "I need to unpack and get some sleep."

When he looked toward the master bedroom she shook her head, reading his mind. "I've already staked my claim on that room."

"Is there another bedroom?"

She shrugged. "Not exactly a bedroom. But there's a loft. I think there's a bed up there."

He glanced up, then without a word picked up his bags. As he did she spotted the sophisticated digital camera and laptop computer. An alarm went off in her mind. "Tell me, Jace Lockhart. Just what is it you were doing while you were traipsing...here and there?"

He settled the strap of the bag over his shoulder. "I reported on the world in crisis. The latest dictator's madness. The latest terrorist bombings."

"You're a reporter?" She was suddenly on her feet, her hands twisting the sash of her robe with furious energy. This was slowly becoming her worst nightmare. Trapped in a cabin with a reporter.

He looked up, wondering what in the world had set her off. "That's right. A TV reporter."

Her tone hardened. "And you want me to believe you just arrived here tonight by accident, without any knowledge of the fact that I was here?"

He didn't bother to hide the weariness in his tone. "That's right. Am I supposed to care that you're here?"

"Are you saying you don't know who I am?"

"Should I? You told me you're..."

She saw the look that came into his eyes the moment he made the connection. Heard the disdain in his tone.

"I guess I'm even more tired than I realized. Oh, yeah, I know who you are. The actress. Even in war-torn countries your face regularly makes the headlines. So what are you doing up here? Slumming?"

"Getting away from people like you. I'm not feeling very friendly toward reporters these days. They've been hounding me unmercifully."

"Isn't that what you Hollywood celebrities thrive on?"

"Some do. I just don't happen to want them in my life right now."

"Right now? Does this mean you're involved in some sordid little scandal?" When she didn't say anything more, he shook his head. "Well, you can relax. I'm not that kind of reporter." His tone hardened.

"Believe me, I'm not the least bit interested in who you are or what you're up to."

"That's what you say now. But when some tabloid TV show offers you a quarter of a million dollars to tell the world that you spent the night with Ciara Wilde, you'll be just like all the rest."

He gave a snort of disgust. "A quarter of a million? You put a pretty high price tag on your scandals, don't you, Hollywood?"

She bristled at the demeaning nickname. "You'll take the money. And you'll give them every juicy little detail you can dream up."

"Like I said, I wouldn't waste my time reporting on some…unsavory Hollywood gossip."

"That's what they all say. But I've been betrayed by too many so-called friends to trust anyone. Do I really look that gullible?"

"What you look like is—" He clamped his mouth shut and gave her a long, insolent look before he turned to climb the stairs.

Stung, she gritted her teeth. She knew what she looked like to men like Jace Lockhart. He didn't have to say it. His expression had said it all. It was something that had been made abundantly clear from the moment she'd arrived in Hollywood. The bimbo. The slut. And all because of the body that nature had given her, and the characters she'd portrayed in her films.

To his retreating back she called, "I don't care who you are or what your connection is to this cabin. I want you out of here in the morning. Is that understood?''

Jace paused. Over his shoulder he said, in a cool, controlled voice, ''As soon as the storm lets up, one of us will be leaving. And you can bet that quarter of a million you think you're worth that it won't be me, Hollywood.''

Two

Ciara huddled under the blankets and listened to the howling of the wind outside the cabin. She'd slept badly. She wanted to blame it on the storm, but the truth was, the fault really lay with the man asleep in the loft. Jace Lockhart. She despised reporters. All of them. But especially those arrogant snobs who thought themselves above the people they preyed upon. They were the worst kind of all. They held themselves above the fray, while selling out anyone they thought beneath them.

She'd seen the look in his eyes when he'd finally figured out who she was. He considered her lower than the characters she portrayed in her movies. Not that she was particularly proud of all the parts she'd played. But she was an actress, after all. She was playing a role, not living it. The trouble was, some people couldn't tell the difference. They expected all actors to behave exactly as their characters did.

She shoved hair out of her eyes and sat up. Now that Jace Lockhart knew who she was, he'd figure a way to use this situation to his advantage. Ambitious reporters like him always did. She could already see the TV news filled with all sorts of unflattering photos of her in the cabin, while news anchors led off with teasers such as "Distraught actress sheds her clothes and her dignity." Or maybe he'd try to seduce her, so that the story would begin "While fiancé frets, actress seeks solace in another man's arms—two weeks before the wedding!"

She tossed aside the blanket and climbed out of bed. At least she was wise to him. She knew all the tricks of his despicable trade. She'd learned the hard way. She was going to see to it that he didn't unearth a single juicy fact that he could twist into a sordid news piece. She'd show Jace Lockhart that she could be as closemouthed and mysterious as he'd been last night.

That air of mystery about him was intriguing. Where had he been, and what had he been involved in these past years? What had happened to make him so reluctant to talk about himself? How had he gotten that scar on his right cheek? Maybe she'd just unearth a few juicy details about *his* past. That way she'd have some ammunition if he decided to attack her in the media.

She slipped into jeans and a T-shirt and tied her hair back into a ponytail. Shivering, she pulled on a flannel shirt for warmth, then crossed to the window and peered out. Her heart fell. The snow had drifted up over the porch, and was still falling. It appeared that, like it or not, she would be stuck here for another day with the smug, superior Jace Lockhart.

With a feeling of dread she opened her bedroom door. It was warmer out here, and she noticed the logs burning in the fireplace. Jace must have fed the fire before returning to his bed. She glanced toward the loft, but couldn't see a thing over the railing.

Grateful for the time alone, she padded to the kitchen and started a fresh pot of coffee, then rummaged through the cupboard until she located a box of cereal. She was just filling a bowl when the door opened and Jace stomped in, carrying an armload of logs.

The sight of him, muscles straining under the weight of his burden, snow dusting his hair, gave her a jolt. She knew dozens of stars in Hollywood who worked out with personal trainers. Not one of them could hold a candle to this man, who looked as rugged and comfortable as though he did this every day.

She watched as he deposited the logs on the hearth. "I thought you were still asleep in the loft."

"Couldn't sleep. Too cold in here." He tossed another log on the fire, then straightened and turned, wiping his hands on his jeans. "I figured I'd better bring in a supply before the entire pile was covered with snow."

She stared beyond him to where snowflakes drifted past the window. "How bad is it?"

He shrugged. "Bad enough that the power's out. A line probably snapped under the weight of all that snow."

She glanced toward the coffeepot and realized it was making no sound. "No power? Now what'll we do?"

"Nothing we can do but wait out the storm. As

long as the supply of logs holds out, we'll be warm enough.''

And stuck, she thought. Stuck together in one small cabin, with no chance of escape. And no hope for any privacy.

She opened the refrigerator and reached for the milk. It was still cold. She started to pour some into the bowl. ''What'll we do about the food in here? Think it'll spoil?''

''I'll carry it out back to the shed. That'll keep it cold and safe from animals.''

''Animals?'' She paused to glance at him. ''What kind of animals?''

''Raccoons. Deer. Their food supplies will be covered by too much snow. They'll turn to scavenging.''

''You don't think there are any...bear in these woods?''

The look in her eyes made the temptation too much to resist. ''I guess they'll be hungry, too.''

''Could they...break down the door?''

''I suppose so. Bears are pretty determined when they smell food.'' He glanced toward the stairs. ''I think I'll be safe enough up there in the loft. But since you hogged the master suite on the main floor, you'd probably be wise to brace something heavy against your door when you go to bed tonight, Hollywood.''

At that precise moment the wind gusted, sending the door slamming open. She gave a yelp and spun around, eyes wide and terrified.

Seeing nothing but the snow, she turned back and

caught sight of his quick, dangerous grin. "That wasn't funny."

"Sorry." He tried to sound contrite. But she could see the smile still tugging at the corners of his lips. "I didn't plan it, but the timing was perfect."

She muttered a couple of unflattering things under her breath as he crossed the room and closed the door, latching it against the tug of the wind.

She turned away and began searching for a spoon. "I must have sounded pretty foolish."

She nearly jumped when he put a hand to her shoulder. His voice was so near, she could feel the warmth of his breath on her neck. "It's the storm, Hollywood. It's bound to get to you."

"Yeah." Even though the nickname irritated her, she couldn't seem to catch her breath, knowing he was standing so close. And she was afraid to turn around to face him. With her back to him she asked, "Want some cereal?"

Was she offering a truce of sorts? He wasn't certain, but he figured he might as well grasp at any straw. "Sure. Thanks. I guess we're going to have to do all of our cooking over the fire now. I saw a grate as well as an aluminum coffeepot for camping in the closet. We can make good use of both of those."

He walked to the closet to retrieve the items. When he returned, he shifted beside her, his arm brushing hers as he filled the coffeepot with water. He crossed the room, placed the grate on the fire and arranged the pot in one corner of the fireplace, over glowing coals. In no time the water was boiling. He added ground beans, and within minutes the cabin was perfumed with the wonderful fragrance of coffee.

Ciara carried the bowls of cereal to the coffee table, while Jace filled two mugs.

He set one in front of her and said, "Just the way you like it. With a pinch of sugar."

She was surprised, and more than a little pleased, that he'd remembered. In all the time that she and her fiancé Brendan had been together, he had never noticed how she liked her coffee. In fact, she'd never seen him fix or fetch anything for himself. He had employees to see to his every need. She couldn't imagine him hauling firewood, or settling for a bed in the loft, or figuring out how to preserve their food once the power went out. In fact, she couldn't imagine Brendan Swift accepting a situation like this without throwing a tantrum.

She sipped, closed her eyes and sighed over the pure pleasure of hot fresh coffee. "I guess being snowbound won't be so bad, as long as we don't run out of logs or coffee."

He chuckled. "If we run out of logs we can burn the furniture to stay warm. But I'm a man who has to have his coffee in the morning. So if we run out of that, watch out."

She couldn't help laughing.

He grinned back and found himself beginning to relax. The thought of being trapped in this cabin with a Hollywood star with an oversize ego had kept him up most of the night. But Ciara was showing a side he hadn't anticipated. She'd accepted this situation with grace. She had a refreshing sense of humor, and was even able to laugh at herself. Maybe, just maybe, they could weather this storm without conflict.

They ate in companionable silence, watching the firelight flicker and dance with each gust of wind that roared down the chimney.

"How long do you think it will take before the roads are passable?" she asked.

Jace shrugged. "We have to wait for the snow to stop first. I doubt they'll bother to send road crews to plow until the storm has blown over completely. We'll just have to hope that once that happens, the spring sunshine does its job on the layer of ice." He shot her a sideways glance. "I'll bet you didn't think, when you left sunny California, that you'd be spending your weekend in a blizzard."

She laughed. "I guess I won't be wearing that bikini I packed."

He quirked a brow. "Listen, Hollywood. If it'll make you feel more at home, you can wear it around the cabin. And I promise you, you won't hear a word of complaint from me."

"That's really noble of you, but I'm sorry. I'm not working now." She picked up their empty bowls and headed toward the sink. "I only wear that uniform when I'm on the job."

"Tough working conditions." He topped off their cups and carried them to the kitchen. "How'd you get started acting?"

She turned and accepted the cup from him, and was disconcerted to find him staring directly into her eyes.

A most uncomfortable feeling, especially since his were deep brown, with a soulful look that did strange things to her heart.

She decided to try to shock him. It was the least she could do to pay him back for that bear scare. "I stripped for the producer." She lifted the cup and took a long, deep drink, satisfied by the lift of his brows. "He liked what he saw, and said the part was mine." There, she thought. That ought to fix him. "How'd you become a reporter?"

Without missing a beat he said, "I stripped for the network producer. She didn't like what she saw and sent me to Bosnia."

Ciara laughed so hard she nearly choked on her coffee. Jace laughed just as hard.

"Okay," she muttered, sticking out her hand. "I think that makes us even."

"For now." He accepted her handshake and absorbed a sudden jolt to his system. There was definitely something about touching her that was downright dangerous. And he knew plenty about danger.

He crossed to the door and pulled on a parka. "I'm going to gather more firewood. And check the shed for a generator."

"A generator?"

"In case this storm decides to hang around. It'll give us enough juice to heat the water and keep the pipes from freezing."

When he let himself out, Ciara carried her cup to the fire and stood staring thoughtfully into the flames. It occurred to her that if Jace hadn't intruded on her privacy, she would be facing this storm alone. The terror she'd felt last night when she'd thought a stranger was breaking into the cabin would be nothing compared to the terror she'd be experiencing right now if she were dealing with this on her own.

She had come here thinking she'd find peace and solitude in the rugged mountains. Then she'd found herself fighting off an intruder. She'd had her moment of panic, especially when he'd overpowered her and wrestled the rifle from her hands. But within minutes she'd been reassured that he wasn't here to do her physical harm. Being trapped in a sudden spring blizzard, alone and unable to go for help, would have left her terrified. She probably would have been pacing the floor by now, consumed with fear and praying for a road crew to rescue her.

For some strange reason she felt safe with Jace here to help her deal with the problems. He had the look of a survivor. There was a toughness about him. And an aura of danger and independence. Wherever he'd spent the past years, she'd be willing to bet it wasn't someplace snug and safe.

Still, she didn't intend to let down her guard. There would be not one word spoken about Brendan, the wedding in two weeks that she'd run from, or her future plans that could be revealed later to the media. She had no intention of forgetting the fact that Jace Lockhart—soulful eyes aside—was a reporter.

After heating water in the kettle over the fire, she washed the dishes and tidied the kitchen. She was just finishing when Jace returned, carrying another armful of logs.

"The snow's letting up." He nudged the door shut with his hip and walked to the fireplace, where he deposited the firewood.

"Did you find a generator?"

"Yeah. Looks pretty old and rusty, but I'll test it later to see if it works. Even if it doesn't, there's enough wood to keep us warm." He added another log to the fire. "I spotted your red convertible out in the shed, Hollywood. It suits you. But it'll be pretty useless in all this snow."

She winced, knowing Jace was right. The little foreign sports car wouldn't make it around the first bend in a road covered with ice and snow.

Jace opened the door, retrieving several empty boxes. "I found these in the shed. We can put the perishable food in them. There's a shelf high enough to keep them out of the reach of most animals."

She started removing some food from the refrigerator. "Except the bears."

He joined her and gave a quick smile. "Ah, those bears. Clever beasts."

Now why did her heart have to do that sudden free fall whenever he got too near? She gathered up the carton of milk and turned, bumping into his chest. Her fingers fumbled and she dropped it. It was only Jace's quick reflexes that kept it from hitting the floor. And all the while, he kept his gaze locked on hers.

"All this talk about bears is going to give me nightmares tonight.'' She knew she was babbling, but she needed to say something to cover her awkwardness.

''Do you get them often?'' He packed the carton in the box and waited while she rummaged about, locating cheese and eggs.

She nodded, sobering suddenly. ''Often enough to miss a lot of sleep.''

''You're not alone.''

''You too?'' She looked up. The laughter was gone from his eyes. In its place was a bleakness that startled her. Her gaze was drawn to the scar on his cheek, and she found herself wondering if that had anything to do with his bad dreams.

She turned away and scanned the contents of the refrigerator one last time. ''I guess that's everything.'' She opened the freezer. ''What about all this?''

He nodded, relieved that she'd changed the subject. ''We'll have to store that in the shed, too. If it starts to thaw, we'll just have to cook everything and have ourselves a feast.''

She lifted out neatly labeled packages and stacked them in the box. When she was finished, Jace set aside two packages.

''I hope you're not a vegetarian,'' he said.

''No. Why?'' She eyed the packages suspiciously. ''What's that?''

''Tonight's dinner.'' He winked, and Ciara's heart did another flip. ''My sister, Mary Ellen, always did have a good eye for prime beef.''

He hefted the boxes and carried them to the shed where he stored them on a high shelf, placing several heavy boards over the top to keep any curious animals away.

Then he began tinkering with the generator. As he worked he found himself thinking about Ciara. She might have teased about packing a bikini, but the truth was, the clothes she'd brought were hardly the Hollywood type. She looked as natural in jeans and a flannel shirt as she did in those sexy, glittery gowns she usually shed in her movies. She seemed different too, from the brainless characters she portrayed. There was a sense of humor beneath the sultry looks. And a sensitivity he hadn't anticipated. Despite her earlier attacks on his chosen profession, she'd instantly backed off when she'd caught a glimpse of his pain.

He turned away, rubbing his cheek. He was reading too much into all this. And spending entirely too much time and energy thinking about Ciara Wilde. She wasn't the problem at the moment. Survival was.

As he stepped from the shed he glanced skyward. The snow had stopped, at least for the moment, and the sun was actually trying to break through the clouds. But if the storm clouds to the north were any indication, there could be more snow on the way. He was determined to keep a supply of firewood beside the fireplace at all times. That way, no matter how much snow fell, they'd be warm.

A short time later he strolled back inside, scraping snow off his boots as he did. Leaning against the door he watched as Ciara poked at the fire before adding another log. The thin fabric of her T-shirt strained against her breasts, and he felt a rush of heat that had nothing at all to do with the warmth in the cabin.

"You're getting pretty good at that."

She looked up, drew her flannel shirt tighter before closing the firescreen. "Yeah. In no time I'll be baking bread and spinning wool into cloth."

"Now those were the good old days." He studied the way her jeans molded to her hips, and decided that he definitely needed to cool off. "The snow's ended. I think I'll take a walk. Want to come?"

She shook her head. "I'd love to. But the warmest thing I packed was a denim jacket."

He pointed to a door off the kitchen. "There are parkas and boots in that storage closet."

She brightened. "I'll just be a minute."

She emerged wearing an oversize parka, the cuffs of her jeans tucked into hiking boots. "Okay. I think I'm ready to brave the elements. Except that I couldn't find any gloves."

They stepped outside and followed the line of trees. Beyond the cabin the grade rose sharply, and they found themselves climbing until they emerged on an open hillside. It was a struggle to walk through all that snow, but the view was worth it. Sunlight glistened on a dazzling, pristine wilderness.

Ciara stopped in her tracks. "Oh, just look at it."

Jace paused beside her, then looked down. Their cabin far below looked like a toy nestled so snugly in the woods; all that could be seen was the smoke coming from the chimney. All around them was snow—so white it was nearly blinding. Distant fences were nearly buried beneath the drifts. It lay heavy on tree branches, dragging limbs nearly to the ground. A branch somewhere snapped beneath the weight, and the sound echoed in the silence like a gunshot.

"You'd almost think—" her voice was hushed, reverent "—we were the only ones to see this."

"We are. Except for them." He pointed and she followed his gesture, then gave a gasp of pleasure at the sight of the herd of deer just emerging from a stand of trees.

She and Jace stood perfectly still, enjoying the image of the graceful animals picking their way through the drifts. Suddenly, one of the deer caught the scent of humans, and the herd bounded away, disappearing into the woods as quickly as they had come.

For the space of a heartbeat Ciara couldn't find her voice. When she did, she managed to whisper, "Wasn't that wonderful?"

"Yeah. Pretty neat." He glanced over and caught the glimmer of tears on her lashes before she managed to blink them away. "Haven't you ever seen deer in the wild before?"

"Not since I was a kid. I never expected to be so moved by the sight. But they're really special, aren't they?"

He nodded. "Come on, Hollywood. Let's lighten the mood. I'll race you to the top of the hill. Last one there cooks dinner tonight."

It would have been an easy run without the mounds of snow. But now it was like running with both feet tied together and heavy weights in their boots. After only a couple of steps, Ciara felt herself falling. As she went down, she managed to snag Jace's arm, dragging him with her.

"Hey. No fair." He fell into a snowbank, and she landed beside him.

"You didn't spell out any rules." She scrambled to her feet and broke into a run. "You just said last one there cooks dinner."

"Oh, I get it." He started after her. "You want to play cutthroat, do you?" When she eluded his grasp, he made a dive, tackling her around the middle. She fell, and he landed on top of her.

A mistake, he realized. He was suddenly all too aware of the soft curves beneath him, and the way his body sank into them. He was playing with fire here.

Unaware of his reaction, she gave a laugh as she struggled free of his grasp and started to crawl away. But he was too fast for her, catching her foot and dragging her back down. When he rolled her over, she had a face full of snow.

"Oh, you're going to pay for that, Lockhart." She scooped up a handful of snow.

Reading her intentions, he ducked his head, and she smeared it in his hair instead. "Bad aim, Hollywood." He bent his head and shook it like a great, shaggy dog, sending a snow shower over her face.

She scooped up another handful and managed to stuff it down the neck of his parka. At his surprised look, she gave a roar of laughter. "Looks like my aim just got better."

"I'll have to do something about that." He caught

both her hands in his and locked them over her head. Then, with a wicked smile, he picked up a handful of snow. As he brought it slowly to her neck he taunted, "Now what're you going to do about it?"

"Jace." She was laughing harder as he began to unzip her parka. "Don't you dare!"

"Dare? Did I hear you say 'dare'? Are you daring me, Hollywood? I think I'd better warn you—from the time I was a little kid, I never could turn away from a dare."

"Jace." She saw the glint in his eye, and started wiggling.

Without warning, he dropped the snow and cupped her face in his hand.

The look he gave her was hot and fierce, as though he was fighting a war within himself. There was strength in him, she realized. And an undercurrent of violence—or perhaps passion. Whatever it was, it frightened her.

And then his mouth was on hers. There was nothing soft or gentle or persuasive about the kiss. It was as hot, as hungry as the look in his eyes. And as demanding.

Jace didn't even know how this had happened. One minute, it was all good-natured teasing. The next, he'd wanted more than anything in the world to taste those pouting lips.

And, oh, the taste of her. At the same time sweet and savory, icy cold and hot as sin. And even now, knowing he ought to back off, he couldn't seem to find the willpower. Instead, he savored the flavor of her and took the kiss deeper. His hand fisted in hair that was even softer than it looked. All silken strands that tangled around his fingers and brushed against his palm, inviting him to take more.

He hadn't expected this softness. It was a surprise. *She* was a surprise. Sweet when he'd expected her to be tough. Vulnerable when he'd anticipated an icy wall of reserve. Everything about her was different from what he'd anticipated.

Ciara's head was spinning. She knew she ought to resist. But there had been no warning. And now, with her senses reeling, she couldn't seem to do more than sigh as she lost herself in the pleasure of his kiss.

There had been so many fake kisses in so many movie scenes, she'd lost count. But this was no act. This was so real, so soul-stirring that she felt her breath back up in her throat. Felt her heart pounding in her chest. Felt herself melting into the snow.

This was a man who knew how to kiss, moving his mouth over hers with a thoroughness that had her sighing. He kissed her as though he were tasting the sweetest of confections. Drinking her in. Feasting on her. Against her will, she lost herself in the kiss, forgetting all her promises to herself to hold this man at bay.

And then, just as her lips softened and opened to him, he abruptly jerked away. She blinked. When her blurred vision cleared, he was already getting to his feet.

Bad move, he decided, as he reached down and helped her to stand. They might be stuck here for days. He'd better keep his hands to himself. The last thing he needed in his life was one more complication. And a woman like this would definitely prove to be a complication.

"Time to get back to the cabin. My hands are freezing." His tone was as flat and unemotional as he could manage over his wildly beating heart. It irritated him to note that his hands were shaking. He stuck them in his pockets and started off at a brisk pace.

"Yeah." Ciara brushed snow from her backside, then struggled to keep up with his impatient strides. If he was going to pretend nothing had happened, she'd play along. In fact, it would be a lot better this way. They'd both pretend this had been nothing more than a moment of weakness, that it had already been forgotten.

"But just so you know, I got closer to the top than you did. So you can make dinner."

Three

Ciara stared around with a look of wonder as they made their way down the hill. "I can't believe this much snow fell in just one day."

"Yeah. These spring storms can be deadly. They're almost worse than in the wintertime. At least then you know what to expect." He shot her a knowing grin. "This time of year you could get caught in your bikini. That *was* a bikini you were wearing last night, wasn't it?"

"A thong. And you're not going to let me forget it, are you?"

"Why should I? It's not something I'm liable to forget."

He was rewarded by a glimpse of Ciara blushing. Not something he'd ever expected to see, especially since she had been so defiant last night. But then, she'd been fighting nerves. Maybe she'd merely tried to cover them with an act of bravado.

"Watch out for these drifts." Jace picked his way through the mounds of snow, breaking a trail for Ciara to follow. In places the snow was so deep that it reached nearly to their waists. Hidden beneath were rocks and stumps and fallen trees just waiting to trip them.

Jace turned to offer his hand, and saw Ciara standing perfectly still, her head lifted, one hand shielding her eyes from the sun.

He followed the direction of her gaze and caught sight of a hawk lazily riding air currents overhead. "Majestic, isn't he?"

She nodded. "He's a beauty. I've always been fascinated by hawks. Occasionally when I'm driving, I'll spot one perched on a light post high above the freeway. I always find myself wondering why it doesn't fly off to the wilderness."

"Maybe there's a girlfriend on a nearby light post. After all, there has to be something keeping him in town."

"Maybe so. But why don't they both fly away? It just seems so much more natural to see one here in the mountains than to see one trying to adapt to life in a crowded, bustling city."

"They're like all creatures." His tone deepened. "Adapt or die."

Ciara nodded. "I guess that's true. We all have to adapt. But look how much we sacrifice for our urban sprawl. Noise and traffic and people in our faces. It just seems a pity that we pay such a high price for civilization."

"Don't be so quick to knock it. I've seen the other side. Primitive life isn't all that pure and noble." Jace's voice hardened. "There's just as much violence in nature, and in small, developing nations, as there is in any big, cold, impersonal city."

Ciara was surprised by the passion in his voice. He

was such a contrast in moods. For the most part funny and irreverent. But maybe he used that offbeat humor to mask much deeper feelings. She found herself wondering once more just what he'd seen, and where he'd seen it. Whatever it was, wherever it was, she felt certain it had been filled with violence and tragedy.

Before she could form a question, a frightened rabbit suddenly dashed across the snow. In a blur of motion the hawk went into a dive and sank its talons deep. The rabbit shrieked in pain, then went eerily silent as the hawk lifted into the air. Within minutes it had flown out of sight with its prey, leaving nothing but drops of blood in the snow to mark its passing.

Caught up in the drama, Ciara could do nothing more than stare into the distance. In the blink of an eye, everything had changed. The pastoral scene had turned into one of frightening violence.

Finally finding her voice, she turned. "How could you possibly know that would happen?"

"I didn't. At least I didn't expect to see it happen right here in front of us. But it was a pretty good bet that our hawk was searching for lunch." Seeing that she was shaken by the incident, he took her hand. It was cold as ice. And the mere touch of her hand in his packed a punch that had him sucking in a breath.

"Come on. We need to get inside where it's warm." He led her over a series of buried boulders.

As they neared the cabin she turned to him. "This morning you mentioned Bosnia. You've been there?"

He nodded. "Bosnia, Kosovo, and half a dozen other towns all over eastern Europe."

"Then you've seen firsthand all the things that the rest of us only saw on the nightly news."

"I've seen enough." He opened the cabin door and stood aside to let her lead the way inside. "More than enough."

As she stomped snow from her boots she glanced over, and noticed that the bleak look had returned to his eyes. And the frown line was there between his brows.

In an effort to lift his spirits she said, "If you'll bring the milk from the shed, I'll make hot chocolate."

"It's a deal." He turned away, eager to escape.

Jace took his time trudging through the snow to the shed. The violent scene with the hawk had triggered an explosion of memories. Of burned-out buildings, and towns under siege. Of the sound of distant gunfire that went on night and day. Of old men and women scavenging food and water and firewood. Of entire families forced to flee with nothing but the clothes on their backs, leaving their homes, their histories behind in search of peace.

Of Ireina. The bomb.

He had thought a visit to this mountain cabin would be a return to normalcy. That he could simply put the past behind him and get on with his life. What he hadn't counted on was the fact that he carried so much baggage. The past was still with him, here in his mind. Haunting him. Taunting him. And the least little spark could set off a firestorm of memories. Some pleasant. A few poignant. All painful.

He paused outside the shed and studied the snowdrifts that reached almost to the roof. Suddenly in his mind he was transported back to that small village outside Bosnia…

In an unexpected downpour, he and his crew had taken refuge in a deserted shed. They huddled around a small fire they'd started on the dirt floor. They had looked up in alarm at the high-pitched whine that signaled an approaching missile. Before they could react, a side of the building was blown away. And with it, their driver. As the rest of the shed slowly collapsed around them, they scrambled free and piled into their truck, keeping one step ahead of the advancing army of terrorists.

The driver—a man from a nearby village—had been young. No more than eighteen. He had taken the dangerous job of driving the news crew in order to help feed his family. He'd had a pretty little dark-eyed girlfriend who had collapsed in grief when she'd heard the news of his death. Jace had learned later that she was carrying the driver's baby; they'd planned to marry. But the war and chaos in their country had prevented them from seeing it through.

That night, as Jace fed the news to the networks, he had been completely poised—his face, his voice, devoid of the emotions churning inside him. He was, as always, the complete professional. Looking back on it he realized he'd never permitted himself to give voice to his grief, choosing instead to push himself to work even harder, to block the feelings.

It was only one of the hundreds of instances in which he'd suppressed his emotions on the job. It was the only way he knew how to survive. But he was only now beginning to realize what a terrible price he'd paid for his stoicism. Though he still couldn't bring himself to speak of them, the scenes of all that carnage haunted him. And something as simple as an attack by a hungry hawk could bring the memories flooding back, casting a pall on the day.

He ran a hand through his hair and realized he was sweating. He hadn't really left any of it behind. He'd brought it all home with him. And he feared it might remain with him for a lifetime.

By the time Jace returned to the cabin, Ciara had added a fresh log to the fire and had set her boots nearby to dry.

As he placed the carton of milk on the counter, she noticed that he had carefully composed his features. But, though he was no longer frowning, there was no warmth in his eyes. Whatever memories he carried, they hadn't been resolved, she thought. They'd merely been tucked away.

Like her, he'd come here to be alone—to think, to bleed, to resolve. And then, hopefully, to move on. But like her, he was forced to snatch what little time he could find alone, to do just that. She wished, for both their sakes, that the snow would melt quickly, so that each of them could find the solitude they sought.

Jace stepped outside and retrieved the rusty generator that he'd hauled from the shed.

"You have a choice to go with the hot chocolate—" she poured milk into a pan and set it over the fire "—plain toast or cinnamon toast."

"That's it? No sandwiches? No soup?" He closed the cabin door and slipped out of his parka and boots.

Ciara grinned. "You can have whatever you'd like. As for me, I wouldn't want to spoil my appetite for that fabulous dinner you're going to make."

"You're not going to let me forget about that, are you?" He spread newspapers over the floor, then knelt and began disassembling the motor.

"Not a chance." She set bread over the coals, turning it often until it was evenly browned on both sides. "After all, it isn't every day I have a reporter willing to feed me."

He glanced over, enjoying the way her hair had escaped from the ponytail to dip provocatively over one eye. "Oh, I bet there are plenty of reporters willing to take you to dinner."

"Sure. And they're all after something. A scoop about a fling with my leading man. A feud with my director. A catfight with some other actress."

He couldn't resist saying, "Not to mention those reporters who would just like to get you into bed."

Instead of disagreeing, she surprised him by nodding. "That too. So they can brag about it the next day. You wouldn't believe how many sharks there are out there who feed on celebrities.''

At the tone of her voice he looked up. ''Sounds like you've been bitten a time or two.''

''Oh, yeah. I've been bitten. But I'll never give them the satisfaction of seeing me bleed.''

''So you came up here to bleed in private.''

''Yeah.'' She thought about it a minute. ''I guess I did.'' She looked over. ''How about you? Any blood left in those veins?''

''Very little. I practically bled to death before I made it here.''

She was surprised, and more than a little touched, by his admission. It had to be difficult for a very private man like Jace Lockhart, who wasn't accustomed to sharing much of his life with others.

''We're quite a pair, aren't we?''

He nodded. ''The walking wounded.''

She crossed the room and knelt beside him, placing the toast and hot chocolate on a tray between them. She nodded toward the generator. ''Do you really think you can fix that thing?''

He shrugged. ''I've never thought of myself as a mechanic. But in a jam, I've been forced to repair a motorcycle engine, a truck's driveshaft, and the broken wires on my sound equipment. Not to mention the time I had to defuse a bomb.''

''A...bomb?'' Her hand went to her throat. ''Where?''

''Myelinore. A town so small it isn't even on a map. I was following the trail of a group of terrorists who had blown up a U.N. truck and had taken a survivor as hostage."

"Why?"

"Because they wanted to get world attention."

"No. I meant, why did you follow them? Why didn't you just report the incident and let somebody else do the tracking?"

"Oh." He gave that quick grin that always did strange things to her heart. "I was the only one around. If I hadn't followed them, they'd have gotten clean away. And the man they'd taken hostage was a friend of mine who had a wonderful wife in Paris, along with two small children. I figured I'd never be able to face Monique and her kids if I didn't do all I could to save Henri."

"And did you? Save him?"

"Yeah. After nearly getting us both killed. When the terrorists left him bound and gagged in a deserted house, I broke in, thinking I'd just untie him and we'd slip away. But the terrorists had very cleverly booby-trapped the place before they left. There wasn't enough time to escape, so I had to figure out which wire to cut or we'd both have ended up like that rabbit with the hawk."

Ciara shivered. It occurred to her that the danger she'd sensed about Jace Lockhart was very real.

"Weren't you scared to death?"

"There wasn't time to think about being scared. I did what I had to."

I did what I had to. Those words triggered a memory of her childhood. She'd once asked her mother how she had kept going, when she'd found herself alone with six children depending on her. And her mother had said, *I didn't have time to feel sorry for myself, honey. I just did what I had to.*

Ciara shook aside the eerie feeling, to concentrate on Jace. "After you'd freed Henri, and had escaped the booby-trapped house, what did you do?"

"We ran as far and as fast as we could, and hid in the forest until we could make our way back to safety."

"Did you ever go back to that town? Myelinore?"

"There was nothing to go back to. When the terrorists were done, they'd blown it clean away. The few buildings that remained were empty. All the residents had fled."

Ciara's voice lowered. "And Henri?"

Jace smiled then, and she could see in his eyes a sense of satisfaction. "He went back home. To Monique and his kids. The last I heard, he was serving as an advisor to the U.N. team in Paris. And living quietly in a cozy cottage in the country." He bit into the toast and shot her a look. "Hey, this is good."

"Of course it is." She sipped her chocolate, still reeling from all the things he'd told her. His life was so different from anyone else's she'd ever known. And so far removed from her life in Hollywood that she couldn't even begin to imagine it. "Why does it surprise you that I can cook?"

"I didn't expect you to be handy in the kitchen."

"I'm not really. But I do know how to make a few

things. Breakfast, mostly. I make a really mean omelette.''

"Good. You can show off your skill tomorrow morning."

"What makes you think I intend to cook tomorrow?''

"Because, if I'm making dinner tonight, it's the least you can do to show your appreciation."

"I think I'll wait until I've tasted your cooking. I may not be so grateful."

"Coward. You're going to eat those words."

"Thanks. But I'd rather eat steak. I'd like mine medium, with a few mushrooms and onions on the side.''

"What you'd like and what you'll get may be two different things." He stopped tinkering with the generator long enough to devour the rest of his toast. Then he downed his hot chocolate in several long gulps. "Thanks. I guess this will hold me until dinnertime.''

"I should hope so." Ciara picked up the tray and headed for the sink. "Because that's all you're getting, unless you make it yourself."

Minutes later, Jace looked up to see her heading toward the bedroom. When the door closed he turned his attention to the generator. He really needed to get this thing in good working order as quickly as possible. He was desperate to restore enough power to use his laptop computer. He'd promised to check in with his wire service as soon as he arrived in the United States. By now they'd be wondering where he was, and why he wasn't bothering to contact them. He didn't want his crew thinking he'd completely deserted them.

But the truth was, he suddenly couldn't work up much enthusiasm for world news. It never seemed to change. When peace came to one area of the world, war inevitably broke out in another. He supposed the world would always be divided between men of goodwill, and men of ill will with a lust for power and domination.

He sat back to study the rusted wires in his hands. But his thoughts kept drifting to the woman in the other room. He'd told her more about himself than he'd intended. Maybe it was because she was so easy to talk to. She had a way of listening. Really listening—not just faking it. And she had a way of asking questions without being intrusive.

He grinned as he started scraping away rust before splicing several frayed wires. Next he'd be trying to convince himself that Ciara Wilde was just like any girl next door. Still, despite the movie star face and fabulous body, there was a freshness about her that was disarming.

Usually he could tell, after just a few minutes with someone, whether or not he wanted to know them better. In Ciara's case, he sensed there was a whole lot more inside than the woman she showed to her public. Maybe, just maybe, he'd reserve judgment. It could be that his first impression had been colored by fatigue.

Or it might turn out that she was "Hollywood," after all. In which case, he'd be only too happy to send her packing as soon as the weather allowed.

Four

In her bedroom, Ciara opened the notebook and removed a sheaf of dog-eared papers. Since she had the luxury of several hours before dinner, she'd decided to use the time constructively. She pulled a chair close to the window for light, then set several candles on the nightstand. Tucking her knees under her, she began to scan the first page, making corrections as she read.

She'd been working on this screenplay for the better part of a year. At first it had seemed an impossible dream. With her demanding schedule, how could she ever hope to find the time to craft a script that was both bright and interesting, with characters who had depth and soul? But little by little it had begun to take shape. She wrote everywhere. Between scenes on the sound stage. During long evenings on location, while the rest of the cast and crew partied. She even wrote on weekends, whenever Brendan was engaged in his own movie projects.

Now that she'd completed several drafts, she had become even more critical. She'd read enough scripts in her time to know that her characters were coming along nicely. The dialogue flowed smoothly. The setting was exactly the way she wanted it. But some of the action scenes still seemed contrived.

She paused, pen between her teeth. *Action.* That was it. That was what was all wrong. She'd been influenced by the sort of action Brendan faced in his movies. Sound effects and computer-generated explosions. Now she found herself thinking about the things Jace had lived through. She'd never before met anyone like Jace Lockhart, who had seen real terrorists, and had defused a live bomb. The mere thought of it had her heart pounding, her palms sweating.

How could anyone live their lives on the edge of danger each day, never knowing what they would have to face next? What would a man like Jace have inside him that would give him the courage, the nerve, to keep going?

She'd seen the televised news segments of the bloody scenes of carnage, when terrorists' bombs had exploded in public places. The sight of the chaos, with dazed victims staggering out of harm's way, was horrible to watch. How much worse must it be for Jace to have lived through it, when the victims weren't strangers, but people he'd known and cared about? How could he keep everything in his life on an even keel, with such images burned indelibly into his mind?

Immersed in the feeling, she bent to the page and began to write, using Jace as her model. Only when the candles had burned too low, and the light outside the window grew too dark to make out the words on the page, did she look up to realize she'd been writing for hours. She carefully placed the pages in the note-book and set it on the night table.

She had often lost herself in her writing. But there were always so many interruptions. These few hours had been like a special gift. No pressure. No schedule. No jarring telephone or fax to mar the silence. No signal from the director to prepare for another scene, or makeup and wardrobe people milling about.

Though it had been difficult at first, she had finally adjusted to having people around her constantly, dressing her, fussing over her hair and face. *Adapt or die,* Jace had said. She nodded. It was true. As alien as it had seemed to her, she had managed to adapt to a life lived constantly in the public eye. But that didn't mean she had to like it.

She stood by the window a moment, staring into the gathering shadows. What would it be like to live like this all the time? To have no distractions? No reporters pushing and shoving to be first with the lat-est tidbits of scandal. No one knocking on her door, telling her it was time for her voice coach, her dance instructor, her personal trainer.

As Brendan often reminded her, she couldn't have it both ways. If she wanted the success and the glam-our and the life-style, she had to accept the publicity, the hordes of reporters and the loss of privacy. But was it worth the price? Whenever she thought about leaving it all behind, she was reminded of the life she'd left. Would that be her fate? She shivered. No. She would never go back.

Money was important to her. Not just because of

the things it bought: the place in Malibu, and the pretty little house in Kentucky that she'd bought for her mother. More important, because it meant security and independence—something Ciara treasured above all else. She'd watched her mother struggle with the burden of six children and a husband who found all his dreams in a bottle. They'd moved from one shabby apartment to another, often leaving in the night when her mother couldn't scrape up enough money to pay the rent. When her father had finally left them, her mother was forced to work two jobs just to keep her family together.

Ciara clutched her hand into a fist, until she forcibly relaxed each finger. She was never going back. If it meant playing empty-headed blondes jiggling in a bikini for the rest of her life, that's what she'd do before she'd go back to the life she'd known as a child. Whenever she thought about leaving it all behind, she would suffer a flashback to her needy childhood. That was always enough to remind her that she couldn't have it both ways.

Still, wasn't it possible to have what she wanted, and reclaim her life? Or would she find her world crumbling, and all her hard-won independence lost?

When she had first voiced her concerns about a lack of privacy, Brendan had been quick to soothe. It was true that he had made a career of attracting the media. And that meant for her, as Mrs. Brendan Swift, whatever privacy she craved would be further eroded. It was only natural to assume that the marriage of two movie superstars would only increase the blinding glare of the spotlight, he'd reminded her. But Brendan had also assured her that the merger of their two fortunes would "buy" them a certain amount of privacy. There was his mansion, of course, which had become such a fortress that the photographers could only snap their pictures from helicopters, unless specifically invited onto the grounds. But Brendan had a reputation for being a freewheeling spender. There were rumors that he spent as much as he earned. And lately she'd begun to wonder if his fortune was really all he led her to believe it was. There was the nagging little fear that he coveted her money, and her fame, as much as her love. When she'd suggested a prenuptial agreement, he had balked, saying that if the press learned of it, he'd look foolish. When she'd pressed, he'd gone into a rage. Hadn't he been more than generous with all his ex-wives? Why wouldn't he treat his current wife even better?

Brendan was so smooth, so persuasive. She felt as though she'd been swept along by the sheer force of his overpowering personality. He'd dismissed her worries and trampled all her defenses. Still, the nagging little fear persisted. Maybe because he'd been too smooth. Too persuasive. And a little too annoyed at her questions.

She'd tried to give him back the engagement ring, telling him she needed time to think. But he wouldn't take it. He insisted that he loved her and that they'd work things out. But he refused to talk about the things that were really bothering her. He wanted to go ahead with the wedding and then work things out afterward. He didn't understand that she just couldn't do it that way. And so she'd run two weeks before her wedding. And was running still. But sooner or later she would have to return for the reckoning. She'd better be prepared with the answers. And right now, she didn't know what they were, what she wanted. All she knew was that she would have to live with her decisions.

She pressed her hands to her temples and rubbed at the headache that was beginning to throb. That's what she got for thinking. But then, that was the reason she was here. To think. To plan. And to come to some decisions, no matter how painful.

Jace was doing some heavy thinking of his own. It helped to have the generator to focus on. But while his hands were busy, his mind was in overdrive. He'd forgotten just how pleasant it was to have an entire day to himself. No agenda. No video or audio. No notes to transcribe. He closed his eyes a moment, listening to the sounds of silence. No traffic screeching. No mobs shouting. No thunder of automatic rifle fire in the distance.

It had been years since he'd been back in the U.S. And even more years since he'd had absolutely nothing more pressing than a generator that required his attention. Why had he resisted so long? If he'd known how soothing, how healing this would be, he'd have been here months ago. Or would he?

Time for a little honesty. Maybe the truth was that he'd been afraid of this very thing. Afraid that if he found life too pleasant, too undemanding, he might not want to return to the wars, the famines, the floods, the assassinations. And then where would he be? Until this past year he'd always known exactly what he wanted. To live life on the very edge of danger. To travel to distant lands. To experience the thrill of discovering something new and exciting just around the corner. Oh, there were times, especially in the past year, when he'd toyed with the idea of settling down. He knew he wouldn't be able to keep up his globe-trotting life-style forever. And the thought that all his friends had become immersed in their own lives, with families of their own, made him feel as though he might have missed something important. But the idea of marriage, of a lifetime spent with one woman, seemed laughable.

Not that there hadn't been women in his life. But all of them, like him, enjoyed a relationship free of commitment. Like him, they'd had demanding careers that filled whatever holes there might have been in their lives. That's just the way he liked it. He'd always needed the freedom to come and go as he pleased.

Jace hadn't been with a woman since Ireina. And he hadn't met a woman who got under his skin enough to make him want to take that leap into happily-ever-after. In truth, he didn't believe such a woman existed. He believed even less in happy endings.

He glanced at the darkened windows and pushed the generator and its parts aside. He'd deal with it later. Now it was time to wash up and cook that dinner he'd promised. He was going to make Ciara Wilde eat her words.

No, he corrected. He was going to make her eat the best steak she'd ever tasted—and sigh in ecstacy over every single bite.

"Umm." Ciara stepped from her bedroom and paused in the doorway. "Something smells heavenly." She glanced toward the fireplace, where Jace was grilling steaks.

He looked up and absorbed a jolt to his system. She was still dressed in jeans and the flannel shirt. But she'd brushed her hair long and loose, and it fell in soft waves to her shoulders. The earlier walk in the fresh air had given her skin a healthy glow. Even without a trace of makeup she was stunning.

The cabin was snug and inviting. Jace had massed candles on the mantel. They cast a soft glow over the room. For the sake of warmth, he'd set two places side by side on the big coffee table, facing the fire. In the middle of the table was a bottle of wine and two stemmed glasses.

Her eyes widened in surprise. "Wine? How in the world did you come up with that?"

He grinned. "I found a well-stocked wine rack in the pantry. Not that I'm surprised. The Fortunes have always enjoyed only the best food and wine. I hope you like merlot." He poured, then handed her one glass, taking the other with him as he tended the steaks.

She sipped. "I can see that you're taking your responsibility as cook seriously."

"Absolutely." He expertly turned the steaks. "That way, when you make breakfast tomorrow, you'll have to work even harder to beat me, Hollywood."

"Now why would I want to beat you? What makes you think I'm the least bit competitive?"

He shot her that grin that always seemed to send her heart into a tailspin. "You're in a competitive business. You'd have to be as aggressive as all the sharks you swim with. Nobody gets as far as you have without fighting hard for it."

She rolled her eyes. "You spend a day with me and decide you know all about me."

"Oh, I don't know everything. Yet," he added ominously. "But I've already managed to observe a few things."

She perched on the arm of the sofa. "Such as?"

He reached for a platter. "You don't want anyone to know that you have a tender heart."

"Ha. A lot you know. I'm tough as nails."

"Uh-huh. You can say that, but I know better. You just pretend to be tough so you can keep that tender heart hidden."

"Why would I do that?"

"So you won't be taken advantage of."

Ciara winced. She supposed it was the journalist in Jace Lockhart that had him trying to fit everyone into neat slots. Still, it was unnerving to have him figure her out so accurately.

She watched him spear the steaks onto the platter,

then open a steaming foil packet and arrange mush-rooms and onions and chunks of roasted potatoes around the edge. She eyed the morsels, and used them to change the subject. "Now where did you find those?"

"Didn't you say you wanted mushrooms and onions?"

"Yes. But I was only kidding. I didn't really expect you to have any."

"Be careful what you ask for, Hollywood. I told you. My sister, Mary Ellen, has excellent taste. If it comes in a can, a box or a package, she has it some-where in this cabin. I thought the potatoes added a nice touch. Don't you agree?" He set the platter be-tween their plates, then reached for the bottle and topped off her glass and his own.

He lifted the glass, sipped, then said, "One more thing I noticed about you."

Ciara tensed.

"You have a brain under all that lovely hair. But you don't let too many people get inside it. Probably for the same reason you hide your heart."

"So I won't be taken advantage of?" Her tone was sarcastic, to hide the nerves that had surfaced.

He nodded. "You need to have the upper hand. It's your armor. You like it when others expect someone quite different from the person you really are."

"You mean the hard-edged, dumb blonde bimbo?"

He heard the bitterness in her tone. "I didn't say that. But you do want to hide behind a mask."

"Why should I?"

"So you'll always be one step ahead of everyone else."

She pressed her lips together. "Thank you for that in-depth analysis, doctor."

"It's just a thumbnail sketch. So far. The in-depth analysis comes later." With a chuckle he put his hand under her elbow. This time he was ready for the electricity that always came when he touched her. But even though he'd tried to prepare himself, it left him shaken.

He guided her to the sofa. "Come on. It's time I softened you up with my specialty—Steak Lockhart."

When she was seated he speared a steak and placed it on her plate, then spooned the sizzling vegetables around it. "First the presentation." He glanced over. "Does it meet with your approval, Hollywood?"

"It does." She breathed in the aroma and felt her mouth water.

"Now for the true test." Jace waited while Ciara cut a small piece of meat and tasted it. "Well?"

She grabbed her napkin and covered her mouth, pretending to gag.

Jace caught her arm. "What's wrong?"

"It's—" she struggled to hold back the laughter, and pressed her napkin over her face so he couldn't see her eyes "—just the worst steak I've ever—"

Eyes narrowed, he yanked her hands down. She couldn't contain herself any longer.

"Sorry. I couldn't resist." She was giggling so hard that she could hardly speak. "Oh, Jace. You ought to see your face."

"You scared the hell out of me. I thought I'd poisoned you."

She wiped at her eyes. "You were so...smug." She choked back another chuckle that bubbled up from deep inside.

He was trying not to laugh, she could see. But the warmth of it was there in his eyes, and tugging at the corners of his lips. "Very funny, Hollywood." He sat back. "Okay. But you'd better be very careful from now on. We're stuck with each other until the roads are cleared. Until then, I could be cooking you a lot more meals. And you never know just what I'll put in them."

"I guess I'll have to see that you taste everything before I do." She picked up her knife and cut another bite of meat. With a sigh she said, "Actually, this may be the best steak I've ever eaten." She glanced over. "But try not to let it go to your head."

He was grinning broadly by the time he cut into his own steak. One more thing he'd learned about Ciara Wilde, which he'd tuck away with the other facts: she definitely had an offbeat sense of humor.

"Now it's my turn to dissect you." She cut another bite, chewed, then said, "You're very secretive. The last thing you want to talk about is yourself."

"Maybe it's because I'm such a dull guy."

She gave him a knowing look. "Oh, yeah. Most of us would be bored to tears if all we could do was have missiles aimed at us while we stay one step ahead of an army of terrorists."

He was forced to laugh at her depiction of his life. "That isn't all I do."

"I should hope not. But the fact is, you're like all reporters. Comfortable with facts. As long as they pertain to someone else. When the topic of conversation turns to you, you'd much rather turn the tables and do an interview."

"Is that what I'm doing?"

She nodded. "Haven't you noticed? Whenever the conversation gets a bit too close, you shut down."

He felt a wave of discomfort. She was right on the mark. And he was already beginning to squirm.

"Like all reporters, you have no problem getting down and dirty, asking questions of others that you'd resent having to answer yourself."

"Ouch." He held up a hand in mock surrender. "I promise I won't do it again."

"Oh, yes you will. It's second nature to you. That's what makes you so good at what you do. You're inquisitive. You want to know what makes everyone tick. You'll put your life on the line to get the facts. You'll go to any length to get your story, no matter who gets hurt in the process. The trouble is, you just don't want to be held under that same microscope yourself."

"I didn't realize I was so transparent."

She smiled. "Oh, you're very good at hiding your feelings. I'd say you've had a lot of practice. In a way, an actor does much the same thing. We're always hiding behind our characters. We're most comfortable when we're portraying someone else. In a way, you're playing a part, too—the part of the dispassionate observer. The trouble with that is, you're not nearly as lacking in passion as you pretend."

"Okay. I'll admit to that much." His gaze roamed her face, coming to rest on her mouth. "I am definitely a man of passion."

No surprise there, she thought. She felt the heat of his scrutiny and was reminded of his kiss. Though it had lasted less than a minute, it had been hot enough to melt the snow, and had left her trembling with feeling. Even now, just thinking about it, she shivered.

He studied her with new respect. "You know something, Hollywood? You have keen insight into people. I'd hate to have you take up my profession. You'd be a tough competitor."

She merely smiled. But she knew he'd just given her a rare compliment. And she couldn't help being warmed by it.

"See, and you accused me of being soft."

"Softhearted. They aren't the same thing."

"And I told you. My heart is as hard as they come."

He tugged on a lock of her hair, forcing her to meet his eyes. His held just a hint of knowing laughter. "You don't want me to expose you for a liar, do you, Hollywood?"

When he twisted the strand around his finger, she felt the sudden spiral of heat all the way to her toes.

She pulled free and reached for her wine. Her throat was dry as dust. And her hands, she realized, were trembling.

Five

"What attracted you to reporting, Jace?"

Their meal had been long and leisurely. And, because they were both struggling to ignore the sexual attraction, they seemed determined to keep their conversation easy and impersonal.

Jace topped off their wineglasses and leaned back, stretching out his long legs to the warmth of the fire.

"As a kid there was a restlessness in me. I always loved nothing better than to ride a horse at breakneck speed over an open meadow. Or to leap off a cliff and dive into a frigid mountain stream. Maybe it sounds reckless, but I've never feared for my safety. I just had to try everything. I have this need to be wild and free. But at the same time, I always loved reading about foreign lands, and I knew that someday I'd have to see every place I read about. When I went off to the University of Chicago, it seemed only natural to major in history and journalism."

"I bet you played football, too." Ciara glanced admiringly at the width of his shoulders.

He grinned. "Yeah. On a scholarship. But I wasn't interested in making sports my life. When it came time to choose a career, there was no contest. I wanted to see the world. And write about my travels. And being a news reporter made it all possible.''

"What brought you back home?''

His smile faded. "I've had a misery overload recently. I needed to pull back for a while and let things heal.'' He absently rubbed his leg, then turned. "How about you? Was your family in show business?''

So much for his story, Ciara thought. Once again he had smoothly turned the tables, deflecting the conversation to her.

"I grew up in a Kentucky coal-mining town. Dirt-poor. My family was as far from show business as you could imagine.''

"Then how'd you get so far so fast?''

"So fast?'' She arched a brow.

"You can't be more than your early twenties.''

"I'm twenty-seven.''

He inclined his head. "Then I'll ask it again. How did you get so far so fast?''

She laughed. "It feels like forever. I started when I was just a kid.''

"I bet you were a beautiful little kid.''

She gave a huff of protest. "Cathy Wazorski was shy and plain. And mostly scared.''

"Cathy Wazorski? That's your real name?'' He was staring at her with a quizzical look.

She nodded, amazed that she had let that fact slip. She'd always been so careful to keep her personal life separate from her public image. In all the profiles written about her, her past and her family had never once been mentioned. And here she was, running off at the mouth—to a reporter!

Maybe it was the wine, but she suddenly realized she didn't much care about family secrets. Jace was easy to talk to. And there had been so few people in her life that she trusted enough to open up to about her personal life.

"So you were a scared little kid. What were you afraid of?"

She shrugged. "Of everything. My father, who was usually drunk. Of losing our home—especially after my father walked out on us. My poor mother worked two jobs to keep us all together, but it was never enough. We moved so many times, I once went to four schools from September to Christmas. My little brothers and I wore hand-me-down clothes from local charities. I never had a lot of friends. I just never felt like I fit in with the other kids in my class. I did have one best friend—Emily Applegate—who is still a great friend to me. She's the one who introduced me to your niece Eden."

Jace was amazed. This was yet another side to her. This poised, beautiful creature looked as though she'd been raised in a life of luxury, with private schools, tutors, and all the trappings of wealth. "So, you were shy? How shy?"

"A real loner. I kept to myself, and took refuge in books and plays and movies. That was my salvation. In my imagination I was always the beautiful, brave heroine who overcame every obstacle to reach the top. Maybe in your dreams you traveled the world, but in my dreams I lived in a mansion and rode in a chauffeur-driven limousine and had hundreds of men groveling at my feet.''

''Nice dream. How did you make it come true?''

She laughed. ''Which part is true? The mansion, the limousine or the men?''

''Looking at you, I'd say all of the above.''

She laughed again. ''I guess that's what most people think when they see a movie star. The truth is, I have to keep working just to keep one step ahead of all the bills.''

''So, you have to pay your bills just like the rest of us. The mortgage on the mansion. The rental on the limousine. But tell me—how did shy, frightened little Cathy Wazorski from Kentucky get to be a Hollywood star in the first place?''

She sat a minute, lost in thought. Then she shook her head, remembering. ''When I was fifteen I sent a photo to a teen magazine contest. It was the boldest move I'd ever made. I really did it because I was feeling so self-conscious. All the other girls my age were small and dainty, and seemed to have perfect figures. And I thought I was some sort of ugly duckling, because I was tall and thin, and had almost no shape at all. My hair was just a mess. Long and curly, always tangled. I couldn't afford to go to a beauty shop, so I used to cut it myself.''

''That doesn't sound like the profile of a beauty contest winner.''

''No, it doesn't.'' She frowned. ''I was so embarrassed, I didn't tell a soul—except for Emily—about entering the contest. Imagine my shock when I won and was offered a contract with a famous modeling agency in Los Angeles. They said they could see something in me. Something that was unusual enough to make me a standout. So I agreed.''

"You left home at fifteen and went to work modeling?"

"By the time I left I was sixteen."

"Didn't your mother worry about letting you go?"

"Sure. She was plenty worried. But by then she had all she could do to keep things together. I convinced her that it was for the best. She'd have one less mouth to feed. And I could earn my own way, and send her a little money when I got settled in. So off I went to the big city to seek my fame and fortune. Whenever I got scared about being on my own—and believe me, I was plenty scared—I told myself it was the only way I'd ever help my mother.''

She smiled. "I remember the first check I ever sent her. Two hundred dollars. She called me up and cried. She said it was like a miracle. I could hear my little brothers shouting and cheering in the background. She said it was the first time she could ever remember looking forward to getting the mail. Always before it had been filled with bills. And now, she wasn't quite so afraid anymore.''

Jace could see the way her smile softened all her features, and put a light in her eyes that made them glow. "That must have given you a pretty special feeling.''

She nodded. "I started saving every dollar I could,

just so I could always hear that joy in my mother's voice. That's when I was encouraged to switch from modeling to acting. But those were pretty rough years in the beginning. I didn't always...make the right choices.''

Jace thought about the films he'd seen her starring in. Most of the plots were forgettable. But he had to admit that the girl in the skimpy clothes had always been worth the price of admission.

Now he tried to imagine a girl of sixteen, being pressured by studios to star in cheap films and bare her body for the sake of big dollars. In her place, how many others would have had the wisdom or the courage to do otherwise?

Ciara grew thoughtful for a moment before saying, "I was given a lot of bad advice. And there were several people who really took advantage of my ignorance. My first agent stole more than half a million dollars before he was discovered. He got off with a fine and a short time in jail. And when he came out, he went right back to handling the careers of other young stars who didn't know any better. And then there was my best friend—not Emily, but a girl I'd met in L.A. and had become really close to..." She paused, frowned. "Well, she's my ex-best friend, because she sold photos of me to a tabloid. Photos she took with a hidden camera, over a period of more than a year.''

Jace's eyes narrowed. "I can't even imagine such betrayal.''

Ciara sighed. "It hurt so much. But I learned from

it. I grew up. Maybe a little bit faster and a little bit harder than I would have liked. But like my mother said, at least all they stole from me was my money and my trust. I can earn more money, and I'll be a lot more careful with those I trust." Her tone hardened. "But I'll never let them steal my soul."

Jace saw the flash of fire in her eyes and studied her with new respect. "That's a pretty remarkable story. I'd say you've been through a baptism of fire, Hollywood."

"I guess that's true." Her voice softened. "And I guess I'd do it all again, if only because I was able to buy my mother a nice house. It's a pretty little place, with flowers in the yard, and a rocker on the front porch." She smiled, remembering the last time she'd gone for a visit. "My youngest brother still lives with her. He's a senior in high school. Two of my brothers are in college, and one's attending law school. Tom, the one closest in age to me, is married and lives just down the street from my mom. I've never seen my family so happy, or so contented."

"That's really nice. And I'm sure it makes up, at least a little, for what you've had to go through."

"It makes up for a lot to have been able to give them the kind of life they have now."

Jace could see the joy that radiated from her. "So, why are you hiding out up here instead of enjoying all that success? I mean, for a woman with a mansion, a limousine and men worshiping at her feet, you should be on top of the world."

She looked away. "I just needed to…sort out a few things."

He immediately regretted the teasing question that had erased her smile. "Well." He picked up an oven mitt and retrieved the coffee from the fire, filling two cups. "You can have it with a pinch of sugar, or with a splash of brandy."

She tried to force a smile to her lips, but it faltered slightly. "I think I'm in the mood for brandy."

He poured a little into both their cups. As he handed one to her he said, "Here's to healing. And sorting things out. I hope this old cabin works its magic. For both of us."

They touched cups, then drank.

Suddenly Jace brightened. "Do you play cards?"

"You mean like…go fish?"

"I was thinking more like gin rummy."

She pursed her lips. "Yeah. I guess I can remember how to play it. We used to play gin when we were kids."

Jace shot her a smile. "When you were a kid, huh? That's even better." He rummaged through a drawer until he located a battered pack of playing cards. "We'll keep it small. A penny a point." He shuffled, then dealt with all the finesse of a Vegas dealer.

"Fine." Ciara watched for a few moments. Seeing the skill with which he handled the cards, she walked to her bedroom and returned with a pad and pencil. "But just to keep you honest, I'll keep score."

"Gin." With a laugh of delight Ciara laid down her hand.

"Not again. You can't have gin again." Jace set aside the cigar he'd been smoking and looked at all the face cards in his hand, mentally tallying his losses. "That's the tenth time in a row. You've got to be cheating."

"Don't be silly. I'm just lucky."

"Lucky is winning once or twice. Not ten times without a loss." He picked up her cards, studied them. With a muttered oath, he tossed them aside.

"Let's see." Ciara tallied the score, then brightened. "You owe me five dollars and seventy-eight cents."

"That's impossible." He circled the table and stood over her, laying a hand on her shoulder as he studied her figures.

She struggled not to react. But she could feel the heat of his touch through her flannel shirt. "See?" She pointed. "Right here. Five dollars and seventy-eight cents. Want to play some more?"

"Not on your life." He reached into his pocket and peeled off a bill and change.

"That's five seventy-five." She held out her hand. "I have three more cents coming."

"Amazing. You not only cheat, but you're vindictive as well."

"Just practical. I pay my debts, and I expect others to do the same." She smiled when he dropped three pennies into her palm.

She stuffed them into the pocket of her jeans and strolled closer to the fire. "I think that's the most I've won in a year."

"A year?" His eyes narrowed as he walked up beside her. "I thought you said you played gin when you were a kid."

"I did." She gave him one of her best wide-eyed looks. "Oh, and a lot of years since then. Did I forget to mention that I play a lot of gin with the crew on the set when we're between takes?"

"Yeah. You did forget to mention that. How often do you play?"

She shrugged. "That depends. During a long, boring shoot, if the director's waiting for the right light, we might play for hours at a time." She fluttered her lashes. "I don't like to brag, but I think I've gotten pretty good at it. There are a couple of our crew who won't even play me anymore. They're like a certain reporter I know who just hates to lose."

"Hey." He closed a hand over her shoulder. "I don't mind losing. But I hate to be conned."

She ignored the little rush of heat. "Who's calling who a con? I saw the way you shuffled. You probably took lessons from a cardsharp."

He grinned. "Yeah. Maybe I did. His name was Aces Malone, and he was one of the best." He caught her chin, lifted it when she tried to look away. "But, Hollywood, when it comes to cardsharps, he can't hold a candle to you."

His gaze fastened on her lips. For one brief moment he thought about walking away. Thought about it, then discarded it. Hell, he didn't want to be noble.

He just wanted.

He lowered his face and brushed his lips over hers.

It was the merest brush of mouth to mouth. But in that instant everything changed.

He felt her stiffen, just for a moment. Then everything about her softened. Her hands—flexing, splaying across his chest. Her lips—opening slightly as his nibbled and nuzzled and tasted. Her sigh—which was little more than a whisper of pleasure that tugged at his heart.

Ciara felt everything speed up. Her pulse—racing as though she'd just jogged miles along the beach. Her mind—crowded with thoughts and images, all of them erotic and confusing. Her heart—filled to overflowing with a need she'd never even known she possessed: The need to be held, to be cherished, to be savored.

Savored. That was what she felt when Jace kissed her. As though he were tasting something so delicious, that he had to have more. And more. It was the same for her. She couldn't seem to get enough of the taste of him. A taste that was wicked and wild. And more than a little dangerous.

She didn't know why, but when he kissed her, she had the feeling that he was interested in her, just for herself. Not for Ciara Wilde, the actress. Just for Ciara, the woman.

Oh, what was the matter with her? He was just a man. And this was just a kiss. But the press of his mouth on hers was doing such strange things to her. She felt giddy and light-headed and wildly exhilarated. Her fingers curled into the front of his sweater and she hung on as he took her on a wild ride of emotions.

His hands at her back moved slowly down her spine, pressing her firmly to the length of him. Tiny splinters of ice curled through her veins as she felt his hard, muscled body imprint itself on hers. She was cold, then suddenly too hot, as his mouth moved over hers, taking the kiss deeper. And then she couldn't think at all. All she could do was feel as she gave herself up to the pleasure.

Jace tried to remind himself that she was an actress. She returned his kisses so thoroughly, so perfectly, because she'd had plenty of time to rehearse. She was, after all, every man's fantasy. But the woman in his arms was very real. Flesh and blood. Such incredible flesh, he thought as his hands made a slow pass down her back, up her sides, until his thumbs encountered the swell of her breasts. He felt the rush of heat, the flash of need. It was crazy to want a woman like this. A woman so far out of his reach. But reason was warring with desire. And her fingers were soft as they slowly moved across his shoulders. And her lips were so tempting as they moved under his, urging him to take more. And the scent of her was clouding his mind, making him think of all the things he'd ever wanted that had been forbidden. She was an exotic flower growing on some lush tropical island. A priceless jewel just waiting to be discovered. A rare treasure that no one had yet found. And she could be his for the taking.

His hands tangled in her hair, drawing her head

back as he took the kiss deeper still. He ached from the need to touch her everywhere. To feel her body move under his hands. He struggled against the sexual tug that was drawing him closer and closer to the edge of something wild and dark and primitive.

The thought of taking her here on the floor had him trembling with need.

"What in hell's the matter with us?" He lifted his head, caught her roughly by the shoulders.

Her breathing was a little too ragged to form a protest. And so she merely stared at him, hoping he couldn't see just how much she'd been affected by this.

"Sorry." His fingers tightened. "The last thing either of us needs is a—complication right now."

Stung, she pulled away. "I've been handling 'complications' since I was a kid. Sorry if that's how you see me." She turned away to hide the hurt.

He swore. "You know what I mean. We both came here to heal. I've never thought of casual sex as particularly healing."

She lifted her head, glanced over her shoulder. "If there's one thing I've learned, it's that there's no such thing as casual sex. I, for one, take it very personally."

That was a direct hit to his heart. His eyes narrowed. "I'll give you this much, Hollywood. You know how to hurt a guy. But at least one of us had the good sense to stop this before it got out of hand."

She flushed with embarrassment. It was true. If he hadn't stopped them, she wouldn't have been able to do it. The truth was, she'd been too caught up in the kiss to have any sense at all.

Jace needed some breathing room. Picking up his parka and his cigar, he headed for the door. "Don't wait up. I'm going for a very long walk."

Ciara waited until the door closed, then threw the oven mitt, against the wall. What was the matter with her? Why was she constantly letting down her guard around this man? She couldn't for the life of her understand what was happening to her.

Her first instincts about him had been right. She couldn't trust him. What was even worse, she couldn't trust herself around him. There was just something about him that made her forget all her promises to herself.

Trust. What a laugh. Hadn't she been betrayed often enough to know that she couldn't afford to trust anyone?

She decided to take out her temper on the dirty dishes, scrubbing and polishing until they were done. Then she found herself doing exactly what her mother had always done when she'd been frustrated. She began dusting, rearranging, until the entire cabin gleamed. That done, she made her way to her bedroom, where she carefully hung her clothes and pulled on the oversize football jersey she wore to bed.

She crawled between the covers, determined to put Jace Lockhart out of her mind. She'd show him that she wasn't affected by him in the least. By the time he came back, she'd be sleeping like a baby.

Six

Ciara tossed and turned in her bed, determined to fall asleep. But the more she tried, the more restless she became. She had heard Jace return to the cabin hours ago. Had listened to his footfall as he'd climbed to the loft. By now he had probably forgotten all about their little scene and was lost in some pleasant dream fantasy.

Why couldn't she do the same?

She punched the pillow and rolled to the other side, squeezing her eyes tightly shut. She wouldn't glance at the little battery-operated travel clock on the bedside table. She didn't want to know the time. It would only make matters worse if she found out she had the whole night ahead of her.

She clenched her teeth. Why was she letting Jace Lockhart get under her skin like this? Just a night ago she'd thought of him as the most revolting of all creatures: a clever, cunning, intrusive reporter. Now she was angry because he'd had the wisdom to keep them both from making a terrible mistake. And he was right. It would have been a mistake to let the passion of the moment carry them along into something they'd both regret in the morning.

But the mere thought of his mouth on hers, of his

strong, clever hands moving along her body, sent a series of tremors skyrocketing through her. She'd never known such fire, such flash, from a single kiss.

It was the situation, she reminded herself. Two people, both struggling with personal turmoil, in close quarters. They were two volatile individuals, bound to explode when things got too hot.

Hot. She kicked off the covers and sat on the edge of the bed. She was flushing thinking about Jace's hard body pressed to hers. She ran a hand through her hair. It was a good thing it was nighttime, so she didn't have to look at herself in the mirror. She wouldn't like what she saw. What kind of woman was she, that she could be turned on by one man, while engaged to another? All right, she argued. So the marriage in two weeks was in question. But she wasn't being fair to either man at the moment.

What right did she have to question Brendan's character, when her own was so lacking? Oh, wouldn't the tabloids have a field day with this if they were to learn of it?

She slipped out of bed and began to pace. She'd come up here to be alone to think. To clear her mind of all the excess baggage, and make some important decisions. It had been a good idea in the beginning. But Jace's arrival had changed everything. This cabin was too small for the two of them. What she needed was to get out of here—now.

She stopped pacing. Maybe the plows would come through in the morning. She smiled, planning her escape. If the main roads were cleared, all she'd have to do was get her car down the lane. The fact that it was more than a mile long, narrow and curving and slippery with a coating of ice beneath snowdrifts that were nearly six feet deep, would make no difference. In fact, Jace would probably be willing to push the car himself just to get rid of her.

She smiled at the thought. Jace was probably just angry enough to do that very thing.

Then her smile faded. She was indulging in silly, childish wishes. The snow wasn't going to magically disappear overnight. And like it or not, she and Jace would have to find a way to get through the next day or two. Together. Not an easy task, if she were to be honest about her feelings. The simple truth was, Jace Lockhart was the sexiest man she'd ever met.

Maybe it was the fact that he was so secretive. He was the proverbial dark, mysterious stranger who fueled so many of the books she'd loved as a child. Unlike most of the men she worked with, he refused to talk about himself. That only made him more mysterious, more appealing. And he seemed completely unaware of his rugged good looks. She worked with men who spent all their time perfecting their looks; when they weren't working out to keep their bodies in shape, they were consulting skin-care specialists or having their hair styled. The very nature of their careers made them self-absorbed. But Jace was natural, unassuming.

Most of all, he was a man of integrity, something she admired above all other traits. The fact that Jace had demonstrated enough self-control to resist taking advantage of their situation made her respect him. And made her even more ashamed of her own lack of self-control. Oh, why did he have to be here, disturbing her rest and adding to her list of problems?

She dragged a hand through her hair and let herself out of the bedroom. Sleep would be impossible now. She was too agitated to even think about going back to bed. She crossed to the fireplace and paused to warm herself. Suddenly, catching sight of the shadowy figure by the window, she let out a gasp.

"Jace." Her hand went to her throat. "You scared me half to death. I thought you were asleep."

He turned, and she caught sight of his tight, angry profile. If possible, he looked even worse than she felt. As though he were pulling himself back from the edge of a nightmare. His eyes were narrow, dark slits. His mouth twisted into a mask of pain.

"I'm sorry." She backed up. "I can see that you'd like to be left alone."

"Yes." He bit the word off. But as she started to walk away, he laid a hand on her arm. "Wait. I'm sorry. I'm afraid I'm not very good company right now. But that doesn't give me the right to send you back to that cold room." He released his hold on her. "I was—" he took a deep breath "—I was just going to get a drink. Care to join me?"

"All right." She felt trapped. On the one hand she hated to remain here, knowing she was intruding on his dark thoughts. But on the other hand, her room was freezing. And she was far too tense to get back to sleep. Maybe a drink would relax her enough that she could face her bed, allowing him some privacy.

He walked to the kitchen and located the brandy and two tumblers, then carried them to the coffee table. He poured and handed one to Ciara, before downing the other in one long swallow. He refilled his glass, then carried it to the window, where he paused to stare into the blackness.

Ciara sat on the sofa and sipped her brandy in silence. She glanced at Jace, wondering where he'd gone in his mind. Wherever it was, it was too painful for words.

He was barefoot and shirtless, jeans unsnapped and riding low on his hips as though he'd gotten up from his bed, too angry and restless to give a thought to anything but getting away from his demons. She studied the hard, corded muscles of his back and shoulders, and could see the way he clenched and unclenched his fist at his side as he stared, unseeing, into the night.

His torment was so real, so deep, she felt herself wishing she knew of some way to help. Instead, she merely held her tongue, watching and waiting, and feeling entirely helpless.

When he finally spoke, he continued staring out the window, his voice tight, angry, as though each word were being torn from his heart. "I told you about the bomb I defused."

"Yes." She waited, tensing for whatever was to come.

"There was another bomb. One I…couldn't defuse. One I didn't even know about until it detonated.''

"Were you—" she nearly swallowed the rest of the question and it came out in a terrified whisper "—wounded?''

He didn't respond at first, merely sipped his drink. And continued to stare outside, thrust back in time to that event. Seeing the blinding lights. Hearing the screams. Smelling the death all around him as the thunderous explosion seemed to split the heavens.

His voice, when he spoke again, was thick. ''When terrorists plant bombs, they do it with an eye to achieving the maximum destruction possible. This was an apartment building used by American television journalists and United Nations personnel. It was detonated before dawn, when the occupants would be sleeping and therefore most vulnerable. There was no warning. One minute, we were sleeping. The next, we were flung about like rag dolls. Some of us on fire. Some of us missing arms and legs.'' His tone lowered. ''And those were the lucky ones.''

Ciara shivered as he lifted the glass to his lips and drank again.

He drew in a ragged breath, amazed that he could speak of this. It was the first time, since he'd been debriefed by the government authorities investigating the terrorist activities, that he'd been able to put it all into words. But now that he'd begun, he couldn't seem to stop himself. It came pouring out.

"There was a woman. Ireina Dubrova. She was a journalist with an international news agency. We'd been colleagues first, and then lovers. She was…torn from my arms. I crawled through the smoke and rubble, calling her name until I found her. She…died there while I held her. Afterward, I spent about six weeks in the hospital. Then I thought I'd get on with my life. But the nightmares…"

He turned then, and Ciara saw the bleak look in his eyes.

"The nightmares come, like the bomb, when I least expect them," he said. "And then I have to go through it all again. The blood. The pain. The…loss."

"Oh, Jace." Ciara was on her feet and hurrying to his side without a thought as to what she could say or do. But she was so overcome with sorrow, all she could do was try, however awkwardly, to comfort him.

She touched a hand to his. "I've never lost anyone. At least not anyone who mattered. But I can imagine how horrible this is for you."

"I thought maybe a change of scenery would help." He tried to ignore the heat, where her hand was touching his. It seemed a betrayal of Ireina's memory, to react to another while speaking of her. But the warmth of a human touch was seeping through the cold. And surprisingly, having someone to talk to helped, no matter how painful the words. "I was wrong. Change didn't help. There's no escaping it. The memories followed me. And they're just as strong here as they ever were."

"You need to give yourself time, Jace."

He gave an anguished sound that could have been

a laugh or a sneer. "It's been almost a year. And I can't seem to move beyond it." He ran a hand through his hair. "How much more time should it take?"

"I don't know." She twisted her hands together, wishing she could offer something more reassuring, but not knowing how. "I just think a year is such a short time to get over something that hideous."

When he turned away, she continued standing behind him. "I wish—I wish you could have the cabin to yourself, so that you'd have the solitude you need to heal." She touched his shoulder, felt him flinch at the touch. "I'm really sorry to intrude on your grief, Jace. My own problems don't seem so urgent, now that I've heard yours. And I promise you, as soon as the roads are cleared, I'll leave you alone."

He closed his hand over hers and squeezed, the only sign that he heard and understood. As she started to pull away he muttered, "Don't go."

She paused, uncertain as to whether she misunderstood. "I don't want to impose."

"You're not. I'd—rather not be alone right now."

She drew in a long, deep breath. "All right." She crossed the room and picked up the bottle, then walked over and topped off his glass. "Why don't you sit by the fire and talk to me."

"What would you like to hear?"

About Ireina, she thought. How you met. When you knew it was more than friendship. How long you were together. But aloud she merely said, "Why don't you tell me about the different countries you've been to.''

He passed a hand over his eyes and leaned back, struggling to pull himself back from the darkness. ''I haven't kept count. My home base has been Bosnia, but I'd have to say I've been in every country in Europe.'' He managed a weak laugh. ''And that's no small feat, considering that some of them are so new, they haven't even had time to change their name or their currency.''

She was relieved to see him smile, no matter how strained. ''How do you communicate? Do you speak their language?''

''Not all of them. But most people can speak a little English. And I can make myself understood in Russian, Polish, French.''

''I'm impressed.''

''Don't be. It's not a big deal. I'm sure behind my back they're laughing at the American who can't manage more than a few phrases.''

''Such modesty.'' She grinned. ''Didn't you ever get homesick?''

He shrugged. ''I was home. Wherever I went, that was my home.''

Ciara shook her head. ''It's just so hard for me to imagine anyone feeling at home all over the world. The times I've been on location to shoot a film I've hated it. Once I was gone for more than two months. I was so glad to get back to my own house, I wouldn't leave it for weeks afterward.''

''Well, maybe if you had to survive under primitive

conditions, your reaction was understandable. How primitive was it? Where was the film shot?''

"Nice.''

"Yeah, that's pretty primitive,'' he deadpanned.

"Well, my villa had only one pool. And the room service was really slow.''

They both burst into healing peals of laughter. Jace leaned back, all the tension seeping away. He'd needed this. Ciara was so easy to talk to, to laugh with, to be with.

"But really, Jace. Didn't you miss hot dogs at the ballpark? Parades on the Fourth of July?''

"Yeah.'' He looked over at her, surprised that her question roused such feelings in him. "That's exactly it. I'd be doing fine, really enjoying my life. But sometimes, when a friend would send me photos of his wife and new baby by the pool, or his kids on swings in the park, I'd find myself wondering if I was missing out on something.'' He set his drink on the table and leaned toward her, his face animated, his eyes alive again. "I'd lie awake at night and wonder if what I was doing made any difference. Would anyone remember the guy who went off to Europe to cover the news?''

"Don't be silly. Of course they—''

He held up a hand. "But I wasn't building anything solid. I had no one who cared if I lived or died. Nobody who would be really shattered if I left. I find myself thinking that the really smart guys are the ones who find that one special person to love, and then spend the rest of their lives loving her, living with her, creating a family together. And then one day their children grow up to do the same thing. And their children. The cycle of love repeats itself, over and over. And they create this history together. A history that continues through the generations. You see? I report on the history, but I'm not making any. Because I've chosen to hold myself apart, and not look for someone who wants to create a history with me.''

''Considering all the messes people make of their lives, yours is probably the wisest course. Think about all those who make the wrong choices, and marry someone who doesn't want what they want. What happens to their history?''

He shook his head. ''They have to absorb the pain and keep on searching. Because love—true love—is what everyone really wants in this life. And all the rest is just window dressing.''

Ciara turned to stare into the fire. ''My mother is still fairly young. But she seems resigned to spending the rest of her life alone.''

''But you see? She isn't alone. She has you and your brothers. So even if her marriage was less than satisfying, it probably gave her what she most wanted in this life. The love and respect of her children. That's her history.''

Ciara nodded as the truth dawned. ''I never really thought about it before. But you're right. She's alone, but never lonely. Her life is so full, with my brothers all around her. And though she misses me, we talk often on the phone. And she cuts out every article she can find about me, and pastes them in a scrapbook.

She says it keeps me close. My brothers and I are all that matter to her. And if my brother and his wife should have a baby—oh…'' Ciara pressed her hands together as if in prayer. ''She'd be the most devoted grandmother in the world.'' Relaxed and suddenly wide-awake, she stood. ''I'm going to pop some popcorn. Want some?''

''Sounds good.'' He capped the bottle. ''I'll make some coffee. I've had enough brandy.''

While she poured the popcorn into a covered pan, Jace reached over her head to set the bottle in the cupboard. She felt his body brush hers, and struggled not to react.

He filled the kettle, then set it aside. ''I've been meaning to tell you, Hollywood.'' His voice was so near, she could feel his breath tickle the back of her neck. ''About this thing you wear to bed. I didn't figure you for the football jersey type. Somehow I expected to see you wearing some frilly thing cut down to here and up to—'' he almost patted her back- side before he caught himself ''—here.''

She turned, and their faces were barely an inch apart. ''I'll remember that the next time I find myself trapped in a snowstorm. I'll be sure to pack something frilly and low-cut, in case I find myself sharing a cabin with a sex-starved reporter.''

''Sex starved? Yeah, that about sums it up.'' He grinned and caught the banded neckline of her night- shirt between his thumb and finger. ''Not that I'm complaining, mind you. About the circumstances, or the nightclothes. I can't remember when I've ever seen anybody look so good in a Dallas Cowboys uniform. You fill it out nicely.''

"Thanks. You don't do such a bad job of filling out those jeans either.''

Though they were both grinning, she was uncomfortably aware of naked chest mere inches away. She could feel the warmth of his body burning through the thin fabric of her nightshirt.

She knew, without a doubt, that he wanted to kiss her. The truth was, she wanted him to. Desperately. But she wasn't prepared to risk it again. Something happened to her whenever Jace touched her. Right now, his fingers at her neck had her heart pounding. She knew he was affected, too. She could see the little pulse working in his jaw. Could actually see the narrowing of his eyes as they focused on her mouth.

It would be so easy to finish what they'd started earlier. All she'd have to do was move a little closer. Offer him what he wanted. A touch. A kiss. But now, somehow, it was different for both of them. There was more involved. After what he'd told her, she knew his vulnerabilities. And he knew hers. One of them had to be strong enough and smart enough to do the sensible thing. And right now, she figured it was up to her—

"The popcorn will be ready in a few minutes.'' She pushed past him and headed toward the fire.

Jace stood where he was, watching the way the jersey clung to her curves as she set the covered pan over the coals. He knew he was playing a dangerous game, but he couldn't seem to help himself. He wanted her. And the more she ducked and dodged, the more determined he felt.

Picking up the kettle, he made his way to the fire, where he added freshly ground coffee. Then he crossed to the sofa and sat, watching as Ciara gently shook the pan. It brought back a pleasant, half-forgotten memory from his childhood: the smells of corn popping and coffee simmering.

When it was ready, Ciara poured the popcorn into a bowl, then lifted the kettle from the coals and filled two cups with steaming coffee.

"Want to take a chance on another gin game, Hollywood?"

She glanced over, grinning. "You're a glutton for punishment, aren't you?"

"I just want the opportunity to win my money back."

"The first rule of gambling is—" she handed him a cup, and sat beside him on the sofa "—never chase your losses."

"And how would you know that?"

"I played a gambler in one of my films."

He popped a handful of popcorn into his mouth. "Yeah, I guess that would make you an expert."

She punched his arm and was aware again of the rock-hard muscles. "We filmed it on location in Vegas. I got a chance to see the business of gambling firsthand. The good gamblers accept their losses and move on."

"Sure. To the next game of chance." He took another handful of popcorn. "I remember that film. *A Toss of the Dice.* You were a gorgeous redhead."

She nodded and seemed pleased that he'd seen it.

He surprised her by touching her hair. "I like you better as a blonde."

She felt a flutter of nerves, and steeled herself against his touch. "Thanks. In my next film I'll be a blonde."

"Is it a good movie?" He picked up his cup and sipped.

She shrugged. "The best thing I can say about it is that it's my last in the contract. Then I'll be free."

"Free to do what?"

"I haven't decided yet. That's one of the reasons I came up here this weekend. My agent is pressuring me to sign another three-picture deal with the studio. But there are other things I want to try."

"What things?"

She looked down at her hands. Her voice lowered. "Things that don't require acting. It's such a demanding and demeaning business. I've watched so many friends lose their identities. They want the fame so badly, they'll do anything to please their studio, their director, their agent. They'll undergo plastic surgery, change their faces or their bodies until they're unrecognizable. They'll take sleazy parts in movies with half-baked scripts. And they're terrified of getting older. Of losing the best scripts to younger actors."

"What about you?" Jace watched as she frowned.

"I can't help getting older. I may only be twenty-seven, but I've already seen my body change. I'm sick of shedding my clothes in pictures. But those are the only scripts I'm given.'' She turned toward him, eyes flashing. ''I'm not stupid, Jace. I know what the studios want from me. But I'm capable of so much more. I don't want to act forever. At least not in these kinds of films. I'd rather have some control. I'd like to write. And maybe direct.''

''You want to write a screenplay?''

''I already have. I've been working on it for more than a year. It's good. Really good. And if I can interest the right producer, and get a director who has the same vision, it would be a wonderful film.''

''With you in the starring role.''

She shook her head. ''I didn't write it for myself. I don't think the audience would accept me in the role. But if I could get this project completed, the studios would have to take me seriously as a screenwriter.''

It was on the tip of his tongue to remind her that she had as much chance of selling her idea to a studio as pigs had of flying. But he could see the fire in her eyes, and was reminded of the scared girl who had left home so she could take care of her mother and brothers. There was just something about her that made him believe she could do anything she set her mind to.

''You know something, Hollywood? I think those studios better watch themselves.'' He picked up the deck of cards and started shuffling. ''You've been swimming with the sharks long enough that you've developed some sharp teeth of your own."

Her smile grew. "You think so?"

"Yeah. Now come on. I need to rack up five hundred and seventy-eight points before I turn in."

She rubbed her hands together and picked up the cards he dealt her. As she drew the first card, Ciara thought about the way Jace had looked tonight when she'd first come out of her room. Angry. Bitter. Destroyed. Overcome with memories almost too painful to bear. Listening to him, she'd realized that her own problems were minor in comparison.

Right now, the man sitting beside her seemed almost carefree. At least for now, he'd managed to put his demons to rest.

"Come on. Play a card. Where's your mind?"

She looked up, grinned. "While I'm feeling lucky, let's add something more to the pot."

"Like what?" He eyed her with suspicion.

"The loser makes breakfast. Deal?"

He stared at her outstretched hand. "Oh, you really think you're going to put one over on me, don't you? You were already supposed to make breakfast, so it's not much of a deal at all. Let's really fatten the pot. Loser makes breakfast *and* dinner."

"All right." She continued holding out her hand.

"You know, I'm going to like sleeping in while you slave over the fire." He caught her hand in his and roared with laughter. "It's a deal, Hollywood. Loser makes breakfast and dinner tomorrow. Now, let's play cards."

Seven

Jace lay in his bed in the loft, listening to the soothing sounds around him. Outside the wind gusted, sending an occasional spray of snow against the windowpane. A dove cooed from its nest under the eaves. He'd spotted three eggs there earlier and figured the poor bird and her mate were working overtime to keep them warm until the unexpected spring snow melted. Downstairs, the flames hissed and snapped as sap from the wood sizzled and the bark ignited. He'd added a log to the fire before coming upstairs a little after four in the morning.

What a strange night it had been. He'd been suffering the worst possible torment when Ciara had first come out of her room. He'd resented her intrusion into his private hell, and had no intention of sharing his misery with her. With anyone. And yet, just minutes later, he'd found himself telling her everything. What sort of magic did this woman have that she could inspire such trust? He hadn't even divulged this much to his own family. Yet there he'd been, telling her the most intimate details of his life.

She was a good listener. She never stopped him to ask inane questions. She hadn't said all the things most people would have said after such a shocking revelation. She hadn't offered him pretty words or empty platitudes. She'd said only that she was sorry. And that he needed time.

Time. That's what the doctor had ordered. But he felt as if time was running out. He had important decisions to make. About his career. His future. He felt frozen in time. Unable to move forward. Unwilling to go back.

Was he ready to return and face the familiar places that brought back so many painful memories? If he did, would he have to live with the nightmares forever?

But if he chose not to go back, what was he supposed to do with the rest of his life? He absently touched a hand to the scar at his cheek. He was forty years old, and he'd spent almost half his life overseas, covering the most important events of the day. Maybe it was time to step back and take a hard look at his life and his options.

He could always get a job as a journalist here in the U.S. Any one of the networks and wire services would be happy to have a veteran reporter who knew his way around the bureaucracy. But wouldn't the news stories seem tame after what he'd been covering for the past fifteen years? And wouldn't he resent having to compete with slick young journalists half his age?

He could teach journalism. There were a number of universities who'd expressed an interest. The thought of teaching at a university level had a certain appeal to him. And there was the book that was nagging at the edges of his mind. Actually, he'd been mentally writing it for years. The plot was all there. And the characters. But he'd not yet put down a single word. He'd always promised himself he'd tackle it when there was time.

No time like the present. But was he ready to hang it all up and start over? Could he really leave traveling the world behind, and settle down in one place? Or was he only fooling himself?

He closed his eyes a moment and listened to the morning sounds. So quiet. No explosions. No automatic weapon fire in the distance. No screams and cries. No sirens wailing. And yet, he always seemed to be waiting for that eruption of sound to break the silence. It had become as much a part of his routine as sleeping in dingy hotel rooms and eating half-cooked food on the run.

He realized with a shock that he was actually enjoying this pleasant break from routine. He liked waking at his leisure, with no deadlines to meet. And he liked having the time to mull over his possible future, without another crisis to interrupt his thoughts. He liked cooking what he wanted, when he wanted.

He heard Ciara's door open, close. The muted footsteps as she crossed the room. The sound of water running as she filled the kettle with water. Within minutes the cabin was filled with the wonderful perfume of coffee brewing over the coals.

He found himself grinning. He'd finally beat her at gin. Of course, he'd taken advantage of her. She'd been bleary-eyed from lack of sleep, but he'd refused to let her go to bed until they'd played the final game of winner-take-all.

She was such a contradiction. Sophisticated and sweet. Simple yet sly. Brandy and popcorn. He chuckled.

Suddenly, he was wide-awake and eager to start the day. He bounded out of bed. He couldn't wait to see her again. He loved having her for a sparring partner. She was just tough enough to fight back, and he liked that in a woman. Besides, he couldn't wait to taste whatever she was going to fix for breakfast.

Ciara stomped snow off her boots and set the items she'd retrieved from the shed on the kitchen counter. She turned at the sound of Jace's footsteps.

"You came to gloat, didn't you?" She eyed him as he descended the stairs, a towel slung over his arm, his shaving kit in his hand.

"And a cheery good morning to you too." He gave her his most charming smile.

He looked even more irresistible this morning— barefoot, shirtless, with a growth of stubble darkening the lower half of his face. His voice was still a little rough from sleep, giving it a sexy edge.

"Starting breakfast, are we? I'll have my eggs over easy, and my toast dry."

"You're not in a hotel, and I'm not your maid. So you'll have whatever I feel like fixing." She watched as he headed toward the bathroom.

She turned away, smiling as she hung up her parka. The truth was, she welcomed the chance to have something to do. She was always able to think better when her hands were busy. And she had way too many problems crowding her mind right now.

She rummaged in the cupboards until she located the proper tools. Then she started dicing ham, slicing onions, grating cheese. It would be tricky making an omelette over the fire. But she figured since she'd already mastered the art of making toast and hot chocolate, popcorn and good strong coffee, she could manage this as well.

While she worked she mulled over her unhappiness with Brendan. Why was she feeling so uneasy at the thought of marriage to him? He was handsome, charming and amazingly successful as the star of dozens of action films.

He was also moody. His temper seemed to rise and fall in direct proportion to his box office numbers. Lately, though he was still able to command millions for each new contract, his films had been slipping in the ratings. She couldn't quite dispel the nagging little fear that he might be hoping to improve his ratings with their marriage. Her own ratings had been going up. Not that she was treated with any respect as an actress. But her films brought in the money, and that was all that mattered to the studio. And she had a following that Brendan had referred to several times. A following he hoped to tap into.

Another thing that worried her was the fact that Brendan was a party animal. He loved nothing more than to be surrounded by his friends, in both show business and the media. No matter how wild the time, he was always the life of the party. A couple of times he'd stepped over the line. Of course, the few times his name had been linked with anything unsavory, his fans had quickly forgiven. But that only made him think he could get away with just about anything.

It was true that lately, aware of Ciara's discomfort with the press, he'd gone out of his way to protect her privacy. Except for the wedding, she thought ruefully. Even then he'd been wildly apologetic, insisting that though he understood her desire for a simple, solemn marriage, he also had to consider the needs of his fans. They deserved to be included in this very important event. Still, the leaks to the press rankled. And she couldn't help wondering if she could ever expect Brendan to put her first. If he couldn't do it for this, the most important event of her life, wasn't it natural to expect that she'd always have to take a back seat to his fans, his career, his fun?

Was it really Brendan that was the problem? Or was she, as Brendan suggested, merely too self-absorbed and selfish to see another side to this? That accusation had really stung. From the beginning of their involvement, Ciara had gone out of her way to consider Brendan's wishes before making any plans. She'd even conferred with his agent before scheduling their wedding date, so that there would be no conflict with his film commitments. And then he'd betrayed her by notifying the press of their plans.

She pressed a hand to her temple to blot out the unpleasant thoughts. They always gave her a headache, and this time was no exception.

By the time Jace stepped out of the bathroom, Ciara had the coffee table set for two and was just sliding the omelette onto a platter. He was wearing jeans and a flannel shirt. His face was clean-shaven and his hair glistened with droplets of water.

"I see my timing is perfect." He set aside his shaving gear and breathed deeply. "If breakfast tastes as good as it smells, I'm going to be one happy man."

"Men and their stomachs." She laughed. "You can pour the coffee while I check on the toast."

She speared perfectly browned toast from the coals and set them on a plate. As she turned, she saw Jace add just a pinch of sugar to her coffee. Her day got a little brighter.

She divided the omelette, and passed him the toast. "Dry. The way you requested."

"What a conscientious chef you are." He took his first bite of omelette and sighed with pleasure.

"Just paying my dues."

He took two more bites before he could slow down enough to talk. "I'll give you a chance to get even."

"You're darn right, you will. And I intend to wait until you're so tired you can't see straight. Just the way you did to me last night."

He set his fork down with a clatter. "Are you accusing me of cheating, Ms. Wilde?"

"Of taking advantage of your opponent, Mr. Lockhart."

He grinned, picked up his fork, and continued eating. "All's fair in love and cards."

"That's war. And that's exactly what this has become."

"Okay." He lifted his arms in mock surrender. "I surrender. At least for now. Truce?" He stuck out his hand.

"Okay. Truce. For now." She accepted his handshake.

A bolt of lightning would have been less shocking. They pulled apart and ate in silence.

Finally Jace sighed. "This is the best omelette I've ever tasted. And to think you did it all over an open fire. Will you marry me and cook my breakfast every day of my life?"

She couldn't help laughing. "It would be a lot easier on you if you'd just hire a good cook."

"All right. Will you give up acting and come to work for me as my cook?"

Her laughter grew. "You couldn't afford me."

He sighed. "You're probably right. But I'd certainly be the envy of my friends. Just think—Ciara Wilde cooking omelettes. Making eggs Benedict. And once in a while, French toast." He arched a brow and gave her a sly smile. "Speaking of French, maybe I could buy you one of those sexy little French maid uniforms."

"Uh-huh. You've got great fantasies."

"And you've got a great body, Hollywood. I can already see you in that little black number. With maybe nothing more than a big bow in back."

She shot him a sideways glance before draining her coffee. "You've been cooped up too long. Your brain's turning to mush. You definitely need to get outdoors and chop wood…or something.''

"It's the, 'or something' I'd like to consider. Want to play in the snow?''

"That does it.'' She stood. "I paid my debt. The dishes are your responsibility.''

"Where are you going?''

"Into my room. To work on my screenplay.''

"Are you sure you wouldn't rather play in the snow?''

She tossed him a kitchen towel and strolled into her bedroom. Over her shoulder she called, "A word of advice. Find an outlet for all that nervous energy.''

"But that's what I was—''

"A *constructive* outlet,'' she interrupted. "One that doesn't involve me.''

"You're turning into a real drudge, Hollywood. You're no fun at all.''

Ciara wandered out of her bedroom, notebook in hand. Hearing a strange sound outside, she walked to the window. Jace had actually taken her advice and was splitting logs. She stood, mesmerized by the sight of him. He'd removed his parka and had rolled the sleeves of his shirt. The muscles of his arms and shoulders rippled as he swung the ax over his head, then brought it biting into the wood with such force that the log split into pieces. Jace set aside the ax and added the wood to the neat pile, then set another log in place and repeated the process.

She felt her throat go dry as she stood perfectly

still, watching. He was so ruggedly handsome, so competent, he took her breath away. In fact, she realized, he was beautiful. Absolutely beautiful. From the slightly mussed hair to the perfectly sculpted body. From those deep, soulful eyes, to that quick, heart-tugging grin.

He'd tease her unmercifully if she ever expressed such thoughts aloud. But it was the truth. And the more she watched, the more she was tempted to feel that strength. To have those muscled arms around her, holding her, stroking her. To have that strong, hard body pressed against her, and that warm, clever mouth on hers.

She stood a moment longer, then spun away, breaking the spell. What was the matter with her? It had to be this enforced idleness. She had run away two weeks before her wedding with no plan in mind except to escape the media circus. But now that she'd had some time to think, she was beginning to fantasize all sorts of crazy things.

One wild fantasy was that she could step back from celebrity life, and actually make it as a screenwriter. The thought of spending long hours like this, alone with her thoughts, out of the spotlight, was the sweetest dream of all. But could she? Could she make enough money to keep herself and her family as comfortable as they were now? Or was she only fooling herself?

She thought of the frightened little teen who had arrived in Los Angeles without knowing a single soul. She'd never told her family of the hellish nights she'd spent alone, crying her heart out, because she'd been scared to death and there was no one she could call on for help. She never talked about the endless modeling sessions, when she'd gone without food for days, living on nothing more than an apple or a box of raisins. She never talked about the strenuous workout sessions to stay in shape. Others saw only the glamour of her life, covered by the press. The movie premiers. The expensive house in Malibu that she'd bought as a refuge from the public, but which had turned into a money pit. She had kept all the fears and all the tears to herself, sharing only the good news with her family and friends.

Could she face a major life change again? She thought she was stronger now. But maybe she was only fooling herself. What if she risked it all—and lost? Who would look out for her mother and brothers then? They'd come to depend on her. How would they survive without her help?

She dropped her notebook on the table and hurried across the room to slip into her parka and boots. What she needed, right this minute, was a brisk walk to clear her mind.

When she yanked open the door, Jace was just coming up the porch with an armload of logs. He gave her a wide smile. "Now that's what I call eager. I guess you missed me, didn't you, Hollywood?" When he caught sight of her face, his smile faded. She was as close to tears as he'd yet seen her. "Hey, what's wrong?"

"Nothing. I just need some air."

He watched as she raced down the steps and headed toward the snow-covered hills. Then he nudged the door closed and deposited the logs on the hearth. After tending to the fire he hung his parka on a hook in the closet and kicked off his boots.

The last of the coffee was still simmering on the coals. He poured himself a cup, held a match to the tip of a fresh cigar, then noticed the notebook on the table. He picked it up, leafed through, and realized it was Ciara's screenplay.

So this was what had occupied her time for the better part of the day. Maybe she was just unhappy with the way it was going. Maybe she'd begun to realize that writing was hard work, and she'd decided to give up the pipe dream and get back to reality. That could be why she'd run off, close to tears.

Intrigued, he settled himself on the sofa and began to read. Within minutes, he set aside the coffee and cigar, too fascinated to bother with even those minor distractions. He had no idea what he'd expected to find. Certainly not this. The characters were so alive, they nearly leapt off the page. The dialogue sizzled. And the setup from scene to scene flowed perfectly. It wasn't just good—it was fabulous. He couldn't stop now. He had to read to the end and see if she could actually sustain the suspense until the final scene.

Ciara climbed to the top of the hill before she paused for breath. When she finally stopped, she was amazed at how far she'd come. The cabin below was completely hidden beneath a canopy of snow-covered trees. All that could be seen was the smoke from the chimney.

Eden Fortune had been right. This place was completely isolated. She could have been in a remote, primitive wilderness anywhere in the world. A glacier in Alaska. Above the timberline in Wyoming. There was no sound but the sighing of the wind. Hers were the only footprints in the snow. She sat down on a half-submerged boulder and lifted her head at the sound of a bird's cry. High above, two crested cardinals happily feasted on red berries that clung to a branch. They were the only spots of color in the otherwise pristine countryside.

While she watched, a squirrel danced along the upper limb of the tree in search of his own berries. And off in the distance was a herd of about a dozen deer. The sight of them warmed her heart as nothing else could have. Though the unexpected blizzard had caught all of these creatures off guard, and had probably caused them more than a little discomfort, they'd adjusted, and survived.

She loved watching the animals. As a child growing up in coal-mining towns in Kentucky, she'd never had the luxury of appreciating nature like this. And, except for the rabbit her little brother had brought home one day, her family had never had a pet. It would have been one more expense for her already overburdened mother.

It occurred to Ciara that at this moment she was thoroughly content. Oh, it was true that the storm had changed her plans. Like the animals, she'd been forced to improvise. But despite the presence of Jace and the temptation he presented, she'd found plenty of time to think. The only trouble was, she still wasn't any closer to a decision. About her career. Or her future with Brendan. But at least she was enjoying this wonderful day, and the sight of all these creatures enjoying it with her.

With a sigh, she stared at the shadows marching in a line down the mountain. She had no idea of the time, but from the position of the sun, just beginning to sink below the line of trees, she figured she'd been gone for several hours. Time to head home if she wanted to make it back to the cabin before dusk.

By the time she'd trudged through the mounds of snow, she was thoroughly chilled, and eager for the warmth of the fire. She scraped snow from her boots, then let herself in.

Jace looked up from the kitchen table, where he was cutting something on a board. "I thought maybe you were walking back to California."

She laughed. "I thought about it. But then I remembered our gin game. If I ducked out now, I'd never get my chance for revenge."

"Good thinking." He watched as she hung her parka and shook snow from her jeans. "I'll bet a hot bath would really feel good right now."

"Oh, why are you being so mean? It isn't fair to tease me like that." She gave a sigh of regret. "What I wouldn't give for a long, hot bath."

"What would you give, Hollywood?"

At the tone of his voice she gave him a sharp look. "Okay. You've got that cat-that-swallowed-the-canary-look. What's happened?'' She brightened. ''Has the power been restored?''

He shook his head. ''Not yet.''

''I should have known. You were only tempting me.'' Deflated, she turned away.

He watched her, letting the moment stretch out, before saying, ''I managed to fix the generator. We can't keep it running for long periods yet, but I was able to hook it up to the water heater.''

''You mean…?'' She ran to the bathroom and tore open the door.

Inside, the room was as steamy as a sauna. The hot tub was filled almost to the top with hot water. Along one side of the tub was a cluster of scented candles, their soft glow reflected in the shimmering bathwater, their fragrance adding to the allure of the scene.

She turned. Jace was right behind her, watching her expression. ''Is this for me?''

''All for you. I've already had my shower, thank you.''

''Oh, Jace.'' She flung her arms around his neck and kissed him.

As she started to pull away, he dragged her back and muttered against her lips, ''Hey, if I'd known you were going to be this grateful, I'd have heated buckets of snow over the fire yesterday and hauled every one of them in here myself.''

A thrill raced along her spine, and she held on to him for a minute more. Though he was still smiling, she could feel the tension humming through him. It was tempting to think she was the cause of it. A part of her wanted to draw out the moment. But a more sensible part of her thought about the bath. As she started to pull away, he startled her by dragging her close and covering her mouth with his.

This time the kiss was neither easy nor friendly. Her smile faded as her breath hitched. His tongue darted between her lips, meeting hers, sending a shaft of heat straight to her core.

She could feel her blood pounding in her temples. Could feel her bones begin to melt as he changed the angle of the kiss and took it deeper.

She leaned into him, wanting to give more. And he took, feasting like a man who'd been starving.

Slowly, ever so slowly, he surfaced. With an effort, he pulled himself back from the edge, forced himself to lift his head a fraction. "Maybe I ought to join you in that tub."

"Uh-uh." Though she spoke quickly, she realized she didn't really mean it. In fact, the thought of sharing a tub with this man had her pulse racing. "You said it was all mine. I intend to hold you to that."

In defense she pulled away, dancing into her bedroom and gathering up an armload of clothes before hurrying back to the bathroom. "I'll make dinner as soon as I've finished. I promise."

"Take your time. I decided to make dinner myself."

She shot him a suspicious look. "Why? Why are you suddenly being so thoughtful?"

"Maybe I just like the way you express your gratitude, Hollywood. I'll expect even more of it when you've tasted my lemon chicken barbecue."

"After giving me this wonderful surprise, you

could fix lemon chicken burned-to-a-crisp, and I wouldn't complain.''

"Just don't forget to be grateful.'' With his thumbs in his pockets, Jace watched as the bathroom door closed behind her. Minutes later he grinned as he heard the splashing of water, following by her sighs and moans of pleasure.

"If you're not careful, Hollywood,'' he shouted, pounding on the door, "I might have to come in there just to see if you're really alone in that tub. From the sounds I'm hearing, I'm beginning to suspect you're filming a porno flick in there.''

"Leave me alone. Go cook your chicken, while I just wallow in this heavenly pleasure.''

She leaned back and closed her eyes. Laughter bubbled up in her throat, and then burst free. What would the tabloids be willing to pay for this bit of information? And how much of her glamorous movie-star image would be tarnished if the readers were to learn that Ciara Wilde had come wildly, gloriously unglued with ecstasy over something as simple as a hot bath?

Still, the thought of sharing this with Jace Lockhart was very tempting. He was unlike any man she'd ever known. A little too dangerous. A little too mysterious. Surprisingly generous. And far, far too clever.

He was getting to her, she realized. With every teasing joke, every surprising gesture, he was softening her up.

Careful, she warned herself. With Jace Lockhart, you could find yourself in way over your head.

Eight

Jace looked up from the fire when the bathroom door opened. Ciara stood framed in the doorway, wearing a bulky terry robe, her hair wrapped in a towel. From the dreamy smile on her face he knew the bath had lifted her spirits considerably. Whatever had been bothering her before her sojourn into the snow, now seemed to have been washed away.

"It's a good thing you came out of there." He tried not to stare at the darkened cleft where her breasts strained against the fabric of her robe. "I was getting worried that you'd gone down the drain."

"I feel like I could. I don't think I have a bone left."

"That relaxed, huh?"

She nodded. "It was such a surprise. Just the nicest gift you could have given me, Jace. Thank you."

"You're welcome." He grinned. "And if you'd like to show your appreciation again…"

She laughed. "Sorry. I'm not that grateful. I'll just need a few minutes to dress. I don't want to hold up dinner."

"Take your time. The biscuits aren't ready yet."

"Biscuits?" She paused in the doorway of her room, and turned. "You're making biscuits?"

In his best Julia Child falsetto he said, "I always have biscuits with my lemon chicken barbecue."

"You're just doing this to make me feel guilty because you're making dinner instead of me, aren't you?"

His lips curved. "Is it working?"

She shot him a sly smile. "No. But keep trying. One of these times it might work." She nudged the door shut with her hip.

Jace turned his attention to the dinner. While he removed the pan of biscuits from the fire, he thought about the way Ciara had looked, all warm and steamy from the bath, tendrils of wet hair clinging to her neck. Though she'd taken pains to cover herself, there was no way to hide that lush body. The sight of her had him reacting like a randy schoolboy.

He paused a moment, staring into the flames, deep in thought. She had the kind of fresh, natural beauty that needed no embellishment. Without any makeup at all, her face was stunning. The more he got to know her, the more he realized that she wasn't at all like the image she portrayed in films. There was nothing flighty or fluffy or silly about her. And she didn't seem at all hung up on her looks. She was disciplined and determined, and devoted to her family. And now that he'd read her screenplay, he realized she had insight and wit and a fine mind to go along with all her natural assets.

He picked up a fork, turning the chicken. He'd been searching for flaws, he realized. Expecting, maybe even hoping, to find reasons to dislike her.

Instead, the more time he spent with her, the more he learned about her, the more he came to respect her.

"And the more I want you, dammit all, Hollywood."

The words, spoken aloud in the silence of the room, caused him to react with a jerk. Grease splattered, burning his hand. He hardly noticed the pain.

Ciara poked her head out the door. "Did you say something, Jace?"

"Just talking to myself."

"Okay." She pulled the door shut.

He stared at the closed door. Until he'd put the thought into words, he hadn't wanted to admit, even to himself, how much he wanted her. Now that he knew it was true, what was he going to do about it?

This was becoming a problem. No, he corrected. *She* was becoming a problem. He wasn't thinking about wanting just anybody. This was a gorgeous movie star who probably had dozens of guys chasing after her. Hundreds. She didn't need to get involved with some washed-up reporter who didn't even know where he'd be going from here. Hadn't she made it perfectly clear that first night that she despised people in his profession? In fact, he thought with a grin, that was too tame a word. She loathed reporters. All reporters.

Maybe that was one more reason why he was becoming obsessed about her. To prove to her that she was as wrong about reporters as he had been about actresses.

Or at least one actress in particular.

He arranged the biscuits in a basket, and speared the chicken onto a platter. Maybe he and Ciara had become a little less antagonistic since that first night, and a little more relaxed in each other's company. But he'd be a fool to confuse that with anything that might lead to their becoming lovers.

But he wanted her. Knowing all that, he still wanted her. The need was gnawing at him, the tension building inside, wearing him down. It was all he thought about when he looked at her. How she'd felt in his arms. How she'd tasted. And how sweet it would be to make slow, lazy, passionate love with her all through the night.

He uncorked a bottle of wine and then filled the kettle and added ground coffee.

"Umm." Ciara stepped from her room and glanced at the steaming platter. "Are you sure I'm in the right place?" She was wearing a plain gray sweatshirt over leggings, her hair damp and curling around a face still free of makeup. "I think I just stepped into a movie set. There's the cozy fire." She glanced at the coffee table, set for two. "The perfect dinner." She turned to see Jace watching her. The hot, hungry look in his eyes had her pausing for just a beat. Then, to cover her feelings, she said with a laugh, "Ah, and the handsome leading man."

"Your leading man had to leave. I'm his stand-in." He crossed the room and poured two glasses of wine, handed one to her.

Their fingers brushed. Just the merest touch, but

the tingling was there. And the quick rush of heat. She took a step back, breaking contact.

"Have you ever thought of acting, Jace?"

"Not since high school, when I was the ghost of Jacob Marley in *A Christmas Carol.*"

"Not much of a part."

He grinned. Took a step closer. "I wasn't much of an actor."

"Neither was I in the beginning." She could feel him watching her in that strange, quiet way he had. It gave her an odd little quiver in the pit of her stomach. But she refused to back up again. She'd show him she wasn't intimidated by his nearness. "I had to learn everything. How to relax. How to forget myself and become the character."

"Who are you playing now?"

She smiled. "Just myself."

"You play her very well."

"Thanks." Without thinking, she touched his arm. "Need a hand with anything?" She felt his muscles tense.

"It's all ready. Come on." His tone was rougher than he'd intended. The mere touch of her had him tied up in knots. "Let's just enjoy our meal."

She took her place beside him on the sofa and sipped her wine, hoping it would calm her nerves. Just minutes ago she'd emerged from the bath feeling more relaxed than she had in days. But things were suddenly strained between them again. Only this time it was a different sort of tension. One she recognized instantly. He wasn't being at all subtle about his intentions. The only trouble was, she was busy fighting the same sort of intentions toward him.

She took a deep, calming breath when he lifted the platter and held it toward her. She picked up the fork and helped herself to a piece of chicken, then slathered honey on a biscuit, all the while aware that he was watching her.

She would keep the conversation light—if it killed her. "If this is tastier than my mama's, you're going to break her heart." She bit, chewed, then gave an exaggerated sigh. "Poor Mama."

He couldn't help laughing. "Sorry to disappoint you. And your mama. The biscuits were in one of those tins in the box out in the shed. All I had to do was arrange them on a tray and heat them over the fire."

"Oh." She placed a hand on her heart in mock relief. "Mama will be so glad to hear that. She always made buttermilk biscuits from scratch. And she vowed nobody could match her talent in the kitchen." Ciara took another bite. "Now, promise you'll never let my mama know I said this, but the truth is, these store-bought biscuits come close."

"You have my promise. Not a word."

She licked away a drop of honey that clung to her lower lip. But when she looked up and saw the way Jace was staring at her, she went very still, feeling suddenly self-conscious.

His tone deepened. "How's your chicken?"

"Wonderful." She drew in a deep breath, then

slowly expelled it. "How'd you learn to cook like this? Especially over an open fire?"

"I've been in a lot of situations that were much more primitive than this. Trust me, when you're hungry enough, you'll eat whatever is available, in whatever manner necessary." He topped off her wine, and their shoulders brushed. The tension between them thickened. "Where'd you go today?"

"To the top of the mountain."

"So far? That was quite a workout."

She nodded. "I needed it. I had a lot on my mind." She moved the food around her plate, then suddenly pushed it aside and picked up her wine. Crossing to the fireplace, she stood staring into the flames. She couldn't bear to be too close to him. He generated too much heat—more heat than the fire.

She cleared her throat. "There's something about cold fresh air and solitude that puts your life in perspective. I took a good hard look at my life, and I'm not at all certain I liked what I saw."

He frowned. "Why do you do that?"

Her head came up. She turned to stare at him. "Do what?" She had to struggle not to flinch at his dark look.

"Put yourself down that way. Your studio wouldn't be chasing after another contract if you weren't making them money."

"Oh, I make them plenty of money." Her voice took on an edge. "And I don't have to act at all. All I have to do is take off my clothes. I've played the same part so often, I could do it in my sleep. Bimbo in Vegas. Bimbo in Paris. Bimbo in Rio."

His tone roughened. "You can't really believe that."

"Can't I?" She lifted her chin. He saw her lower lip tremble before she turned away. "When you hear something often enough, you learn to say it first, before someone else beats you to it."

He was across the room in quick strides. He touched a hand to her shoulder. "I'm not saying it."

"You're just being too polite. I saw how you looked at me that first night, when you realized who I was. You might not have said it aloud, but you were thinking, 'Oh, yeah, Ciara Wilde. The blonde who does all those bikini movies.'"

"Okay. Maybe I did." He kept his hand on her shoulder and could feel a ripple of tension humming through her. "But that was before I got to know you."

"And now that you know me?" She stared into his dark eyes.

"I intend to get to know you a whole lot better than this, Hollywood."

He felt her stiffen and pull away. "You won't like what you find."

His tone hardened. "There you go again. Putting yourself down."

"I told you. It's easier if I say it first. Then it doesn't hurt as much when others laugh." She lifted her glass and drank, wishing she could swallow this painful lump in her throat.

"I'm not laughing."

"You thought the same as all the others when we met."

"I told you. That was then. Now..." He took the glass from her hand and set it on the mantel. Then he turned her to face him. "Now I know you're so much more than that sexy image on the screen."

"You mean the real me isn't very sexy?"

"You're sexy as hell. And you know it."

She struggled to ignore the tremors that rocketed through her. "Oh, I don't know. Maybe I really am a good actress and this is all just an act."

He shook his head. "I've had plenty of chances to watch you. How you deal with things falling apart. The lack of privacy. The lack of heat and electricity. The lack of hot water." He brought his hands to her shoulders and began gently massaging the knot of tension. "You've managed to take it all in stride. That's not acting."

"That's just a need to survive. It's called..." She saw his gaze center on her mouth. Knew that he was going to kiss her. Felt her throat go dry a second before he lowered his face. "...desperation."

He swallowed the word with a kiss that was so hot, so hungry, it rocked her back on her heels.

"No," he whispered against her lips. "This, Hollywood, is pure desperation."

This kiss wasn't like before. His other kisses had been tentative, testing, tasting. Exploring uncharted territory. And purely spontaneous. But this was bold, possessive. And absolutely deliberate. Not so much taking as demanding. A kiss that drained her, then filled her. And she gave without thinking. As eagerly as he took.

She couldn't seem to catch her breath as she responded to the urgency of his kiss. Her fingers curled into the front of his shirt, pulling him to her. And then all she could do was cling.

The hands gripping her shoulders were almost bruising as he dragged her against him and plundered her mouth. She felt the rush of heat. The quick, jittery charge to the system as his mouth almost savagely moved over hers.

She knew better than to give in to this. It was madness. Nothing more than cabin fever. She knew nothing at all about Jace Lockhart, except the few things he'd been willing to share. And yet here she was, tempting herself with him. But what else could she do, when he was so good, so very good, at seduction?

Oh, and she had wanted this so desperately too. This rush of pure adrenaline, while that hard, muscled body tempted and aroused her.

She moaned as he changed the angle of the kiss, took it deeper. Her blood heated and pulsed, and her breathing became ragged as his hands—those strong, clever hands—began moving over her.

She knew she ought to fight him, but she was tired of holding back. Tired of trying to stay one step ahead of him. Now it seemed all she could do was flow with the feelings. And the feelings that were rushing through her system had her offering her lips with the same hunger as his.

Arguments crowded her mind. All of them negative. What did she know about this man? About his past? And what did he know about her, except what he'd read? She was playing a dangerous game. And he could very well be playing her for a fool.

For the space of a moment she felt a flash of fear. She drew away a little. "We can't...do this."

"Why not?" His big hands framed her face and he stared down at her, while his thumbs traced the outline of her lips. "There's no denying what's between us. It's been there from the beginning."

"But we—hardly know each other." She held herself perfectly still, afraid to move. Afraid that if she even breathed too deeply she would shatter like fragile glass. The feelings pulsing through her were too overpowering. The need too great. She was surprised, and more than a little frightened, by what she was feeling. "This is—" she struggled for breath "—too fast, too sudden. I...can't think."

"Yeah. Thinking's a problem." He combed his fingers through her hair and drew her head back. "It's time we both quit thinking and just allowed ourselves to feel."

"That won't solve anything." Her voice was a little too tight.

"Maybe not. But it'll go a hell of a long way toward sweeping away all this tension between us. And besides, it'll make us feel so good."

"Tension is...normal when you're feeling—" she swallowed "—what we're feeling."

His eyes narrowed on her. "What are you feeling, Hollywood?"

She backed away, her hands fisting at her sides. "You know exactly what I'm feeling. And you're the reason why."

"You mean..." His grin came, quick, dangerous, sending her heart on a fast, bumpy ride. "You're seriously tempted? Are you saying you want me?"

It was on the tip of her tongue to deny it. But she knew he could see through her lie. "You know I do."

His heart started racing. "Well, that makes it a little easier. We both want the same thing. So, what are we going to do about it?"

"Nothing." She backed up another step, until she felt the wall behind her. "You said yourself you don't believe in casual sex."

"There's nothing casual about what I'm feeling." He moved closer, his eyes gleaming in the glow of the fire. "You know something, Hollywood? I've always known exactly who I was and what I wanted. And when I wanted something, I always went after it with absolute focus. But this time..."

She tensed, aware that he wanted to kiss her again. But he held back.

He kept his hands at his sides. "Ever since I came up against you, I seem to have lost all my bearings."

"You're not the only one." She made a sound that could have been a laugh or a sob. It stuck in her throat, threatening to choke her.

"So." He kept his eyes level on hers. "What are we going to do about this? The choice is yours."

For a moment she said nothing. She stared into his eyes. Her throat felt parched. She ran her tongue over her lips before she managed to whisper, "It would help if you'd touch me, Jace. I need you to touch me."

He was afraid to touch her. Afraid that if he did, he wouldn't be able to stop. The need was too great. And the feelings pulsing through him right now would probably turn him into some kind of savage.

"I don't think that's a good idea. Unless, of course, you want the same thing I want."

She brought her hands to his wrists. She could feel the tension humming through him. Could feel the strength of will as he held on to his control by a mere thread. But even as she ordered herself to get a grip on her emotions, something seemed to take over. Something stronger than common sense. The mere touch of him had her sliding her hands along his arms, feeling the muscles bunch and tighten under her fingers. It was exciting to feel the keen edge of tension throbbing through him, and to know that she was the cause.

She couldn't seem to stop herself now. She lifted her hands higher, to his shoulders, then slowly encircled his neck. Despite her fears, she had an overpowering need to kiss him again. She couldn't bear to wait another moment to taste him. She had to stand on tiptoe to reach his mouth. She heard his quick intake of breath in the moment that their lips touched.

It was the merest whisper of mouth to mouth. A

soft little butterfly kiss. But the feelings that pulsed through him shattered all his defenses.

His voice was rough with frustration. His eyes narrowed. He lifted his hands again to frame her face. ''If you keep this up, Hollywood, I'm going to lose all control.''

''Really? That might be…interesting. I think I'd like to see the very cool, very contained Jace Lockhart step out of character.''

''You know what they say. Be careful what you wish for.'' His head was spinning. The whisper of her breath against his mouth was as fresh, as clean, as a mountain spring. She smelled of soap and water, and just the merest hint of some half-forgotten fragrance from his childhood. She had him tied up in knots. And all he could think about was tasting her. All of her. Here and now.

''I remember how you looked that first night.'' The image of her flashed through his mind. Wild-eyed with fear, but ready to stand her ground. ''If I take you, I'll want you like that. Frightened and bold. Advancing and retreating. Demanding and surrendering. And naked. With even those bits of silk and lace gone, so I can touch and taste and feast to my heart's content.''

The thought of all the things he wanted to do with her, to her, had the blood pounding in his temples. He pulled her head back sharply, his fierce eyes steady on hers. ''So, do you still want to see me out of control?''

If he expected to read shock or censure in her eyes,

he was mistaken. What he saw was pure sensuality, mingled with a hint of doubt.

But all she said was, "I might be mildly interested."

"Not good enough, Hollywood. I need your full involvement in this, or I step away."

Though she said nothing, the look in her eyes was too much of a challenge. Besides, his blood was already hot, pumping through his veins with such intensity that he could hear it roaring. Still, he had to give it one more try. For both their sakes.

"It's your call, Hollywood. And if you're smart, you'll run to your room now, and lock the door."

She swallowed, and the sound seemed overloud in her ears. "What if I don't?"

"At least have enough sense to be afraid."

"Are you, Jace?"

"Scared to death." But he knew if she tried to keep him away now, he'd tear her door from its hinges to have her. His head was already lowering until his mouth was fully on hers. The flash of fire caught him by surprise. And then he could feel the need twisting, turning, churning inside.

Against her mouth he muttered, "You should have run when you had the chance, Hollywood. Now it's too late."

"It was too late the minute I walked into this room tonight."

"Yeah." He pressed his mouth to hers, lingering over her lips until he heard her moan with pleasure. "You got that right."

He was through fighting it. He would have her. All of her. He would taste her until he'd had his fill. And touch her everywhere. And if, in the morning, there were regrets, he'd deal with them then. For tonight, he would have everything he'd ever wanted. And in return give her all that he was capable of giving.

Nine

His hands moved over her, and she felt her desire rise as he cupped her hips and dragged her roughly against him. And still he lingered over the kiss. With lips and teeth and tongue, he took her on a wild ride. One minute she was holding on tightly, afraid of falling. The next she felt herself stepping over the edge of a mountain, falling, falling, then suddenly soaring.

While he explored the wonders of her mouth, she drank him in. He tasted dark and mysterious. The tang of cool wine and the sharp bite of tobacco. She sighed. A man of so many moods and even more secrets. And she was determined to learn all of them. Who he was. And what he was. But for now...

All she could do was hold on.

Annoyed with the barriers between them he tugged the heavy sweatshirt over her head, only to discover a chemise of silk and lace beneath. The contrast surprised and aroused him. In the firelight her skin was pale and smooth, like the underside of a rose petal. He was fascinated by the long, sleek column of her neck. He ran his tongue down the length of it, before pressing his mouth to the sensitive hollow of her throat.

She made a sound like that of a purring kitten and

arched her neck, giving him easier access. He remained there, pressing light, feathery kisses along her throat, across her shoulder, over her collarbone. But when he brought his mouth lower, to close over one erect nipple, she felt her knees buckle.

The only thing that kept her from dropping to the floor was his hands, pinning her against the wall. Hands that moved over her body with all the skill of a musician, playing her as though she were his instrument.

In the firelight she looked to him like a goddess. All golden hair and honey skin. Her eyes a little too wide. Fear, he thought, and that knowledge made him bolder. He dipped one hand beneath the waistband of her leggings and tugged until they joined her sweatshirt in a heap at their feet. Then he found her, hot and moist.

Stunned, she could only clutch at him as, without warning, he drove her to the first glorious peak. She had no time to recover as his mouth moved over her body, making her hum with needs she'd never even known she possessed.

Trembling, she reached a hand up to unbutton his shirt, sliding the fabric over his shoulders so she could touch him as he was touching her. She felt a ripple of excitement as her fingers traced the taut muscles of his chest, then moved lower, across the flat planes of his stomach, until she reached the snaps and zipper at his waist. With one quick tug he stepped out of his jeans and briefs.

"Jace." She struggled to see him through the haze

of passion that clouded her vision. But all she could see were his eyes, dark and dangerous, stripping her soul bare, just as his hands had stripped her body.

"This is just the beginning, Hollywood. You wanted to see me out of control." He gathered her against him and dropped to his knees, dragging her down with him. "Before this night is over, I'm going to take you where you've never been."

The darkness, the danger, excited her. She touched a hand to the scar on his cheek, then pressed her lips to the spot. "I don't care, Jace. As long as you go there with me."

They came together in a kiss that spoke of hunger, of need, of blinding, desperate passion. The world beyond this cabin no longer mattered. The wind blew, tossing a spray of snow against the walls, causing sparks to leap and dance in the fireplace. The fire burned low, leaving the cabin chilled. The candles on the mantel sputtered, and threatened to go out with each gust of wind. But the heat between them grew, until their breathing was labored and their bodies were slick with sweat.

No one had ever touched her like this. With lips and tongue and fingertips. One moment, so gently that she wanted to weep. The next, creating a frantic rush of almost desperate need that had her pulse speeding up, her breath racing from between parted lips. Taking her higher. Faster. And farther. Until she lay steeped in pleasure.

She didn't think it possible to be any more satisfied than he'd already made her. But she was wrong.

His movements slowed. He brought his mouth to the silk and lace of her chemise, running his tongue over the edge of her breast, around the peak, until she thought she'd go mad from wanting. He moved the fabric slowly upward, his thumbs tormenting her as he freed her breasts from that final thin barrier. But in his haste to find her skin, he couldn't strip it away fast enough, and he ripped it from her. The sound of the shredding silk broke through the stillness.

At the unexpected sound she cried out, "Jace, wait!"

"Too late. I have to touch you. Taste you. Now."

They lay on the floor, with only their clothes beneath them for a cushion. There was a sofa just a few feet away, and a bedroom just beyond that. But they might as well have been a million miles away. Neither of them could stop—even for a moment—the swirl of passion that held them in its thrall.

Jace thought of all his fantasies since he'd first seen Ciara Wilde on-screen. But none of them could compare with this flesh-and-blood woman. She lay in his arms, weak with pleasure, drugged with passion. Moonlight spilled through the window, turning her hair to flame, her eyes to the color of a storm-tossed ocean. It mirrored the storm raging within him. He could do with her as he pleased. Her sighs of ecstasy were because of him. She shuddered from his touch. The name she cried out was his. That knowledge fueled his passion.

The thought of taking her, hard and fast, made him tremble. He was desperate for release. But he wanted more. There was so much more he had to give. So much more he wanted to take.

He teased her breasts, until she moaned and writhed beneath him. He lifted his head, his eyes deep and unfathomable as they studied her. He watched her lovely expressive face in the flickering firelight. Saw the way her lips parted, her mouth forming his name, though no words came out. Her arms lifted weakly to encircle his neck, and she dragged his head down for one long, lingering kiss.

He knew if he waited much longer he'd go mad. And still he held back, wanting to see her eyes glaze with desire. Wanting to drive them both to the very edge, and beyond. And he did. With lips and tongue and fingertips he brought her to an even higher peak.

She was wonderful to watch. Her eyes were huge, fixed on him, as she gave herself up completely.

She was his, he realized. Only his.

And then he knew he could hold back no longer.

When at last he entered her, she let out a cry. She had thought she had no more to give. But now, half crazed with desire, she wrapped herself around him, needing to hold him to her, needing to move with him, needing to match her strength with his.

He hadn't expected this. This firestorm of passion as they came together. "Look at me, Ciara." His voice was hoarse.

Her eyes widened, and she struggled to focus on him through a burning mist of passion. "Jace." His name was torn from her lips. She shuddered.

And then they knew only this incredible strength.

Their breathing was labored as they moved together, strong and sure, and climbed higher and higher. They were beyond words now. Beyond thought. Beyond anything of this world, as they felt themselves shattering, splintering into tiny fragments and soaring among the stars.

"That was—" Jace paused for breath, amazed at how difficult it was to find his voice "—incredible."

They lay, still joined, their bodies slick.

"Umm." Ciara couldn't manage more than that. She felt as if she'd survived a storm. And in a way, she had. One unlike any she'd ever experienced. She felt bruised and battered. Dazed and disheveled. And completely, utterly satisfied.

Jace raised himself on his elbows and gazed down at her, loving the way she looked, hair damp and tangled, lips still swollen from his kisses. "Am I too heavy for you?"

She opened her mouth, then decided it was too much effort to speak, and merely shook her head.

"Good. I'm not sure I could find the energy to move." He couldn't remember the last time he'd felt so disoriented. Had the earth actually moved? Before tonight he would have scoffed at such a thought. Now...

He traced the outline of her lower lip. "You're an amazing woman, Hollywood."

She lifted a hand to brush the hair from his forehead. "You didn't call me that a few minutes ago."

"I didn't?" He frowned, trying to remember. He

felt as if he'd survived an earthquake—the ground had definitely shuddered. "What did I call you?"

"Ciara. It was the first time you've ever spoken my name."

"Ciara." He whispered it like a prayer. And realized why for so long he hadn't been able to say it. "It's almost too beautiful. Like you."

She smiled. "You think I'm beautiful?"

"Come on. Don't act so surprised. You have to know what you look like." When she shook her head, he persisted. "What do you see when you look in a mirror?"

"I see that plain little girl from Kentucky who had few friends and was always wearing hand-me-down clothes."

She tugged at his heart, in a way she'd never understand, and he could never explain.

He lowered his face and brushed his mouth over hers. Against her lips he murmured, "Then let me tell you what I see." He rolled to one side, and gathered her into his arms as tenderly as if she were that sad little girl she'd described. He cradled her against his chest and stroked, soothed. Pressing his lips to her eyelids, he said, "I see eyes that, when they're glowing with happiness, could melt glaciers." His voice warmed with unspoken laughter. "And when they're iced with fury could freeze the sun ."

"Ah. The old evil eye. It's a look I've perfected over the years. I'm glad you've noticed."

"You bet I have." He dropped a quick kiss on the tip of her nose. "I see a nose that's cute as a button, but can be lifted higher in the air than a proper Boston matron when someone crosses swords with you.''

"I don't lift my—"

"Not yet, Hollywood. It's not your turn to talk." He brushed a light kiss over her lips. "I see a mouth that's full and generous. Really quite kissable. And quick to curve with laughter. It can also turn into the most delightful pout. But, when fighting tears, it trembles ever so slightly."

"My lips don't—"

He kissed her into silence. "They tremble. And it breaks my heart." He ran a finger over her chin. "You have a jaw that juts like a boxer's when you're ready to fight. Which isn't often, thank heavens."

He lifted her hand to his mouth, taking the time to kiss each finger, then pressed his lips to her palm. "I see hands that aren't afraid to get dirty for the sake of hard work. Especially if that hard work means an easier life for the people who depend on you. Your mother and brothers are very fortunate to have someone like you looking out for them."

"Oh, Jace." The gesture was so unexpectedly tender, it had her catching her breath on a sigh. She pressed her forehead to his and took a moment to compose her thoughts. Then she wrapped her arms around him, pressing herself firmly against the length of him. "How do you know me so well?"

"I've spent a lot of time watching you, Hollywood. Which is a pretty pleasant task, considering how easy you are to look at."

"I just don't think anybody's ever seen through my

defenses before. Or ever seen me in quite the way you do.''

"Good. I don't think I want anyone else seeing you like this. Because where you're concerned, I think I could become a very jealous lover."

"Lover. Umm. I like that word."

"Yeah. I kind of like it myself." He ran a hand possessively along her spine, amazed that he was fully aroused once more. How could it be possible to want her again so soon? He had thought that once they got the tension out of the way, things could become more relaxed between them. But if anything, he wanted her more. Once would never be enough where Ciara was concerned, he realized. She was the kind of woman a man would want again and again. She could become a habit. An addiction.

"I'd like to think I'm seeing you in a way nobody else ever has or ever will."

She could feel his physical response and was thrilled and a little awed by it. Drunk with power, she ran slow, lazy kisses along his throat, then lower, across his chest and stomach, then lower still, until she heard his moan of pleasure.

She gave a little laugh of delight. "Maybe it's time to reveal a few more of my deep, dark secrets."

"Careful, Hollywood. You show me too much too soon, I may go into cardiac arrest. Didn't your mother ever tell you it wasn't nice to tease a man like this?"

"Tease? Oh, I intend to do a whole lot more than tease."

"Stop. I can't take much more."

But she wasn't listening. She was already busy driving them both far beyond madness.

"Hungry?" Jace drew a cover over both of them to ward off the chill. Sometime during the night he had carried her to the sofa, where they lay in a tangle of arms and legs and twisted blankets. Though it was barely wide enough for one, they managed to snuggle together, perfectly content with the arrangement.

"What do you have in mind?"

He shrugged lazily and lifted a lock of hair from her eyes. "I don't know." He allowed the strands to sift through his fingers, thinking how soft they felt. Softer than silk. In fact, everything about her was soft. And warm. And exotic. "But I noticed that you hardly ate any of your dinner."

"I think I was too troubled to eat."

"What was troubling you?"

She laughed. "I don't remember. The minute you kissed me, I forgot everything. Including my name."

He pressed a kiss to the tip of her nose. "You've just described what happened to me. I was really worried about my reaction. Now I'm glad to know I'm not alone in this senility."

He glanced idly toward the hot coals that gleamed in the fireplace. "I was going to surprise you with a special dessert. But now it's ruined."

"You were?" She snuggled closer, absorbing his warmth. "What was it?"

"Baked apples. Now they're a couple of blackened cinders."

"Sorry to spoil your surprise. How about some coffee? Is there any left?"

He shook his head. "It all boiled away. I could make a fresh pot."

"No." She put a hand on his arm. "Don't leave me. I don't need anything. Just you."

"Umm. I like the sound of that." He loved the way the gentle curves of her body fit so perfectly against him. Like the missing pieces of a puzzle. Complete. *He* felt complete.

The thought startled him. Now where had that come from? He'd never before needed anyone to make him feel complete. Being alone didn't equal loneliness. All his life he'd been content to be a loner. A man who could pull his own weight, see to his own needs. Leave when he wanted to. Stay if it suited him. Live the way he wanted. He felt a sudden flash of alarm, then took a deep breath and told himself to relax. This changed nothing. They were just…good together.

Annoyed with the direction of his thoughts, he started to draw away. "Maybe I'd better add another log to the fire."

"No need. I'll warm you." She drew him close and pressed her lips to the hollow of his throat.

Against her mouth she could feel his pulse jump, and then begin to race like a runaway freight train. "My, my, Mr. Lockhart. A bit nervous, aren't you?"

"Yeah." He grinned. "I'm not used to having someone kiss my neck. It tickles."

"Really? You mean—" she already had her fingers

crawling over him, teasing his chin, his neck, his chest "—you're ticklish?"

"Knock it off, Hollywood. Don't even think about—"

With a devilish laugh she rolled slightly, straddling him, and bent low to press kisses across his throat, along his shoulder, down his collarbone. Her hair swirled forward, teasing his chest. "What else aren't you used to? Where else are you ticklish?"

He grabbed a handful of her hair and lifted her head. "Careful, Hollywood. This could lead to all kinds of dangerous things."

"Ooh. I just love a dangerous man." She laughed and began to move over him, until, with a moan, he caught her roughly by the arms. In the blink of an eye he rolled them both over and began savagely devouring her mouth.

The laughter died in her throat as the kiss deepened, and his hands—those quick, clever hands—began to work their magic.

His eyes were hot and fierce as they locked on hers. "What is it about you? What the hell have you done to me?"

"I think it's something we've done to each other. Whatever it is, I don't want it to end."

"Yeah. Me neither."

And then he was taking her down, down once more into that dark, murky world of unleashed passion and desire. A world they had only begun to explore.

Jace lay watching Ciara as she slept in his arms. He loved looking at her. The way her lashes cast spikey shadows on her cheeks. The way her lips pursed, as though remembering his kiss even in sleep.

He leaned close, studying her flawless skin, and felt a hitch around his heart. She was quite simply the most beautiful woman he'd ever seen. If he had a lifetime, he would never grow tired of looking at her.

If he had a lifetime. What a foolish thought. They had, at best, a couple of days. Then both of them would go their separate ways.

The thought brought a shaft of unexpected pain. In his whole life he'd never been bothered by goodbyes. In fact, leaving had always meant the start of a new adventure. Something he'd always anticipated more than a kid at Christmas. So why was he letting this get to him? Why was he agonizing over the lack of time? Why couldn't he accept this as merely another new thing to be savored, enjoyed, before moving on with his life?

Ciara's lashes fluttered open. She studied him a moment before saying, "Regrets?"

"Don't be silly."

"Then why this?" She touched a finger to the frown line between his brows. "Do I make you so unhappy?"

"Of course not. It isn't you. It was just a thought."

"Not a very happy one, from the way you look."

He shook his head, wishing he could dispel the mood that had begun to set in. "No. Not a happy thought."

"Maybe this will help." She twined her arms

around his neck and drew him down for a long, slow kiss. "Mmm. Good morning, Jace."

"'Morning, Hollywood." He could already feel the heat beginning. The slow gradual simmer that began deep inside, then radiated upward to his loins, then pulsed through his veins until the blood in them flowed like lava. It was becoming a familiar ritual.

All through the night they had loved, then slept, then loved again. Each time it had been different. At times hot, furious, impatient, with all the frenzy of a summer storm. Other times slow and easy, like old lovers who knew each other's bodies as intimately as their own, and who had all the time in the world to enjoy them.

"Did that help?" she whispered.

"Oh, yeah. The unhappy thought is completely wiped from my mind." He plunged his hands into her hair and stared into her eyes. "The only problem is, now I have a new thought."

"Does it make you sad?"

He shook his head and brushed his mouth lightly over hers. "It just makes me hungry."

"There you go again. A man and his stomach. Always thinking about food."

"I wasn't talking about that kind of hunger." He nuzzled her lips, then the corner of her mouth.

"Oh." She brightened. "The other kind. The good kind."

"Yeah." He traced the outline of her lips with his tongue until she sighed and opened her mouth for him. "The best kind."

"You have a very devious mind, Jace Lockhart. I like the way you think."

"I'm glad you feel that way. Because my brain has affected other parts of my anatomy."

"I've heard it said that men think with—other parts of their anatomy."

He chuckled, low and deep in his throat. "So, would you like to see what I'm thinking?"

She opened her mouth to reply, but he swallowed her words with a kiss so filled with hunger that it startled them both. And then he took her on a long, slow journey, determined to make whatever time they had together as satisfying, as perfect, as possible.

Sunlight stabbed at Ciara's closed lids. She yawned, stretched, then watched as Jace, naked, fed logs to the dying fire. He had such a beautiful body. She loved watching the play of muscle across his shoulders as he lifted each log and set it just so, building the fire with the same quiet competence that he did everything else.

"Good morning," she called. "I can't believe I slept this late."

"'Morning, sleepyhead." He glanced over his shoulder. "We both slept in. The thing that finally woke me was the cold." He turned, started toward her. "I'm afraid I was so busy with…other things, I neglected my duty and let the fire burn down to practically nothing but ashes."

"That's all right. I had my love to keep me—" The words died in her throat as she caught sight of the long, puckered scar that ran from his hip to his ankle. She sat up and covered her mouth with her hand, but not before she let out a cry. "Oh, Jace. How did you…?" She saw him grimace, and instantly regretted her reaction.

She struggled to keep her voice emotionless. "I'm sorry. That was careless of me. It's just that I didn't have a chance to see your scar in the dark. I guess this is a souvenir of the bombing?"

He nodded.

She caught his hands and drew him down beside her. "It looks like it must have been horribly painful."

He rubbed his leg, feeling the ever-present ache. "The doctors have done all they can. They said I just have to be patient and give it some time."

"How bad was it?"

He shrugged. "Severed a few nerves and tendons. There'll be some permanent numb spots. But at least they saved the leg."

Her gaze flew to his face. "You mean, you were in danger of losing it?"

He nodded. "It was a possibility. Things looked grim for a while. It took a lot of therapy, but I managed to walk out of the hospital under my own steam. That's more than I can say for a lot of the other survivors. Some weren't so lucky." He wouldn't look at her. Couldn't. Because he couldn't bear the look of horror and revulsion he knew he'd see in her eyes.

"Oh, Jace."

She shocked him by pressing kisses along the

length of the scar. All he could do was watch as she kissed him with such tenderness. Then she drew him close and kissed his scarred cheek, before pressing her mouth to his.

Against his lips she murmured, "I'd give anything if I could take away your pain."

He clutched her shoulders and drew her a little away, staring into her eyes. "Do you know how incredible you are?"

She blinked. "Why do you say that?"

He shook his head. "You really don't know, do you?" He let out a long, slow breath. "I've been afraid to have you see this. It's so ugly, most people would be sickened by the sight of it and would have to turn away. But you...you not only look at it, you try to kiss away the hurt."

"I would if I could."

For the space of a heartbeat he studied her. Then on a sigh he drew her close and covered her mouth with his in a kiss so hot, so hungry, it robbed her of breath.

"You just did, Ciara." He laid her down and covered her body with his. And as he pressed kisses to her eyes, her nose, the corner of her mouth, he whispered, "By whatever magic you possess, you've managed to do what all the doctors and all the medicines couldn't. You've managed to erase all my pain."

Ten

"Here. Let me get the door." Ciara, arms laden with food from the shed, hurried up the steps and nudged open the door for Jace, who trailed behind her carrying an armload of logs.

"I'm starving." He dropped to his knees on the hearth and piled logs on the burning coals.

"No wonder." She peeled off her parka and immediately began rummaging through the cupboards. "It's almost time for lunch, and we're just thinking about breakfast." She began breaking some eggs into a bowl.

"That's all right." He glanced over and gave her a smoldering glance. "I had better things on my mind this morning."

She laughed. "And I must say, Mr. Lockhart, you have a very inventive mind."

"You're not so bad yourself, Hollywood." When the fire was blazing, he hung his parka, then came up behind her, wrapping his arms around her waist. For a moment she paused to lean back into him while he pressed his lips to her neck.

"Why don't I make the coffee, while you're scrambling those eggs?"

She shivered. His kisses made her knees go weak. "Good idea."

Instead, he brought his hands under her sweater and began to move them upward until they covered her breasts. "Maybe I have a better idea."

Her body reacted instantly to his touch, but she managed a laugh. "That idea kept us on the sofa all morning. Remember?"

"Are you complaining?"

"Complaining? Far from it. But my stomach is. I'm really hungry, Jace."

"Yeah. Me too. But I thought..." He nibbled her neck. "I thought I'd just feast on you a little longer."

She sighed. "Any longer and we'll both starve."

"All right, spoilsport." He lowered his hands, and pressed a kiss to her ear. "Guess I'll make that coffee."

He sauntered across the room—like a rooster, she thought. She couldn't help grinning as she finished scrambling the eggs.

"How about the toast?" he called from across the room. "Want me to make some? Or would you prefer more biscuits?"

"Toast is fine." She carried the skillet to the fire and began gently stirring. "You know, primitive living isn't all that hard."

He shot her a look of surprise. "You call this primitive? We have enough firewood to last a year or more. We have cupboards stocked with every conceivable food. We have comfortable beds..." He saw her grin and added, "Okay. We even have a not-so-comfortable floor and a very narrow sofa. But tonight, I promise, we'll try the bed. And,'' he went on, "with the help of our temperamental generator, we even have an occasional warm bath. That's a far cry from primitive. Just think what our ancestors felt like when they first had to chop the wood, then hunt the game, spin the wool into cloth, sew the clothes, tan the hides, and—''

Laughing, she placed a hand over his mouth. "I get the picture. And I promise, I'll never again call this situation primitive. But I'm not so sure that word wouldn't apply to someone I know who actually seems to be thriving on all of this.''

He nodded as he carried the toast to the coffee table. "I think you're right.'' He filled their cups with steaming coffee, then sat down beside her and bit into his eggs. "I can't say I liked the idea of having the power cut off. But being cut off from civilization isn't all that bad. I thought at first I wouldn't be able to stand not knowing what was going on in the world.'' He gave her a sideways glance. "It's the reporter in me. I'll admit I'm a newsaholic. But the truth is, I think I needed this complete break from the outside world. Without all the interruptions and distractions, I've had plenty of time to think.''

"About what?'' She broke off a piece of toast, spread it with strawberry preserves.

"About where I've been. And where I'm going.''

"Have you come to any decisions?''

He sipped his coffee. "Not so far. But I've certainly been able to work through a lot of things that have been troubling me." He studied her over the rim of his cup. "And right now, thanks to you, Hollywood, I'm feeling like I could take on the entire world. And win."

She almost blushed. "Tell me about your world, Jace. The one you've been living in as a reporter."

He shook his head. "I don't think you want to know about some of the things I've seen. The wars, and bombings, and the misery of the people who've been forced to live through them."

She realized he didn't really want to talk about that part of his life. It was still too painful. "But you must have seen some warm, loving, moving events as well."

He nodded and smiled. "Just when I'd begin to lose hope of ever seeing anything uplifting, I'd witness something that was so noble, so generous, it would bring me up short and remind me why I was there. I wasn't supposed to cover only the sadness, but to report on the greatness of people, as well. Especially people under fire. That's when they're at their best and their worst." He paused a moment, lost in thought. "There was a little girl. No more than six or seven. Long blond curls. Big sad eyes. She'd lost a leg in an earlier bombing, and used a stick for a crutch. Every day I'd see her hobbling through the town where I was reporting on the rebel activity. She'd duck behind buildings at the sound of gunfire, and scurry out of the way of the rebels' trucks. But always she would cross the town square, and return hours later. One day I stopped her and asked her about herself. She explained that she'd lost her father and mother, her older sister and two little brothers— all in the same bombing that cost her her leg. She was now living temporarily with a neighbor family who were good to her, even though they could barely afford to feed their own children. I asked her where she went everyday. And she said she was going to school. There was a woman who taught a few orphans across town, and this little girl went there faithfully. When I asked her why she would risk injury, even death, to go to school every day, she said simply, 'Because I promised my mama before she died that I would not neglect my education.'"

He shook his head. "Months later, when I was in that hospital bed, fighting to walk, I used to think about the courage of that little girl. Some days it was the only thing that kept me trying to get back on my feet."

Ciara swallowed the lump in her throat. "I wonder what happened to her."

"She's been adopted by a family in London."

Her head came up. "How did she get to London?"

Jace shrugged. "I arranged to have her airlifted out of Bosnia before I left."

"Oh, Jace." Ciara brushed her lips over his cheek. "And you try to make yourself out to be such a tough guy."

"Yeah." His voice was gruff. "I'm really a pushover. Especially for long blond curls and big sad eyes. Just don't let anybody else know my secret."

"It's safe with me." Her gaze fell on a notebook,

half buried beneath the cushions of the sofa. "Is that mine?"

Jace picked it up, handed it to her. "Yeah. Your screenplay, Heartbeat."

She arched a brow and looked at him with a quizzical expression. "How do you know the title?"

"I read it. I figured you wouldn't mind, or you wouldn't have left it lying there when you took off for your walk."

She'd forgotten all about it. She got to her feet, feeling as if the cabin had suddenly become too warm.

"What's wrong?" Jace stood and put a hand on her arm.

"Nothing. I just wasn't ready to let anyone else read it yet. Especially someone who earns his living by writing."

"Is that what's worrying you?" He closed his fingers around her arm, holding her when she tried to pull away. "For what it's worth, I thought it was fantastic."

She turned. Studied his face a little too carefully. "Are you just saying that to make me feel better? Come on, Jace. I can take the truth. No matter how bad it is."

"And I'm telling you the truth. It's a fabulous script. I couldn't put it down."

For the longest time she merely stared at him. Then she said softly, "You mean it, don't you? You really, really mean it?" Her eyes started to fill, and she had to blink hard.

He drew her close, as much for himself as for her. Seeing her emotions so close to the surface reminded him how much this meant to her. Despite all her success as an actress, this was an entirely new challenge, and she was feeling vulnerable. "Believe me. When I first met you, Hollywood, I never would have thought I'd be saying this. But you're one hell of a gifted writer."

"Oh, Jace." She buried her face in his shoulder and held on until she managed to compose herself. Then, pushing away a little, she took a deep breath and gave him a radiant smile. "I want to celebrate. I saw some skis in a closet. Let's clear away the dishes, then hike to the top of the hill and ski down."

"Are you sure that's what you'd like?" He glanced at the sofa. "If you'd rather stay in here where it's warm, I could think of some way to celebrate, and get our exercise at the same time."

"Yeah, I just bet you could." She laughed, feeling happier than she could ever remember. There was a lightness around her heart that hadn't been there in years. "Come on. I'll wash. You dry."

"The last time I saw this much snow was in Lake Tahoe." Ciara paused at the top of the hill to catch her breath. She carried a pair of skis over her shoulder. "I was skiing in a celebrity charity event."

"I suppose you're called on to do a lot of those things."

She nodded. "Too many to count. Certainly more than I can possibly accept. But I try to attend as many as I can. It's one of the best things about my business. I realize the importance of using celebrities' names to raise money for good causes.''

''Are you a good skier?'' Jace paused beside her and planted his skis in the snow.

''Pretty average. But I've taken enough lessons so that I don't embarrass myself in public. How about you?''

He nodded. ''There wasn't a lot of time, with all the assignments I accepted. But whenever I could, I'd slip away to Switzerland or Germany. It's some of the best skiing in the world. Have you ever skied the Alps?''

She shook her head. ''It looks so incredibly beautiful in photographs. But there's never been time between movies.''

''Yeah. Time. We never seem to have enough of it. At least not for the things we really want, do we?'' He caught her hand in his and linked their fingers. ''I'd love to show you the Swiss Alps. There's a quaint little resort there. Nestled in the valley between the most majestic mountain peaks you'll ever see. You'd swear you've stepped back in time. Feather beds tucked under snow-covered eaves. Hot toddies served by white-gloved waiters. Warm towels when you step from your bath. And late in the afternoon, just as the sun is going down, you can take a sleigh ride over a breathtaking mountain pass.''

''Oh, Jace. It sounds heavenly.'' Her eyes took on a faraway look. ''You make me realize how much

I've missed in my life. And how much I still want to see and do."

He nodded, growing pensive. "We always tell ourselves we'll do all these special things later. But for some, later will never come."

Ciara could see that he had gone somewhere in his mind. A dark place where she could never follow. She watched, silent and understanding, while he stared into the distance, lost in thought.

At length he shrugged off the mood and brightened. "Well, this may not be Switzerland. But it's all we've got. So come on, Hollywood. What are we waiting for?"

He snapped on his skis, and she did the same. She slipped on a pair of sunglasses, and stuck her hands into mismatched mittens that she'd found in the back of the closet. Then she shoved off and started down the hill. Her hair, which she'd pulled into a ponytail, streamed out the back of her baseball cap like a streak of golden sunlight.

Jace shoved off, too, forging his own trail, until they were skiing side by side. He glanced over to see her laugh with delight. When they approached a line of trees, she veered right and he veered left, and for some time they were each alone, with only the sound of their skis cutting through the snow. Below the tree line, they came together again, smoothly skimming the unbroken snow, until Ciara lost her balance and took a tumble, landing in a drift.

With a look of concern Jace retrieved her ski and came to a sudden stop beside her. "Are you okay?"

"Yeah." She yanked off her mittens and glasses, then accepted the ski from his hands. "The tip of my ski hit something. A boulder, I think."

"But nothing's broken?"

"Nothing but my pride."

"Want to finish the run?"

"Of course I do. You don't think I'd quit now, do you?" Her cheeks were as red as apples, her eyes bright with challenge. "In fact, if you'd like, we'll race the rest of the way."

"Suits me. What's the prize for the winner?"

She gave it a moment's thought. "Do you think the generator will work long enough for another hot bath?"

"I think that can be arranged."

"Well, then, I think the loser should have to scrub the winner's back. And then, while the winner is soaking up a very long, very hot bath, the loser can fix dinner."

"Hmm. I like the sound of that. It's been a long time since I had my back scrubbed."

"Oh, you're so confident. I like that in a man. But I hope you're not too disappointed when you're fixing dinner again tonight." She stood and fastened her skis, then picked up her glasses and mittens. "We'll go on the count of three."

"Hurry and get those mittens on, Hollywood. I can't wait for that back scrub."

Minutes later they flashed down the hill in a blur of color.

* * *

"A little lower." Jace closed his eyes and sighed with contentment. "Ah. Now that's just about perfect."

Behind him, Ciara knelt in the steamy water and moved the washcloth slowly over his back. Though she made all sorts of noise about hating to lose, the truth was, she was having the time of her life.

The tub was filled almost to overflowing. With each movement, water sloshed and threatened to spill over the edge. It was deliciously warm and fragrant—although she had lost the race, she'd won the right to use bubbles.

At first Jace had refused. "I think it's only fair that the winner should decide what kind of a bath it'll be."

"I agree. But if you've never tried a bubble bath, how do you know if you'd like it or not?"

"I want a simple, manly bath. Plain old soap and water. I have no intention of smelling like a French—" He stopped and burst into laughter at the look on her face. "You know what, Hollywood? You can pout better than anyone I've ever known." He'd kissed her lips, then stepped back. "Okay. We'll try it your way. Maybe a bubble bath won't be so bad."

With a squeal of delight she'd poured a generous supply of liquid into the tub, and turned the taps on as high as they'd go. Now they were practically drowning in bubbles.

She caught a handful and smeared them over his shoulders before touching her lips to the back of his neck. "Now, aren't you glad you gave in? There's nothing like a bubble bath, is there?"

"Especially when it's shared by two. Lower."

She moved the washcloth down his back, and he gave another sigh.

Ciara studied the hard muscles of his back, the ripple along his upper arms and shoulders. "Beautiful," she whispered. "Absolutely beautiful."

"What is?"

"Your body."

"Uh-huh. You're just trying to distract me so I'll forget about the back scrub. Lower."

She moved the washcloth lower, and without thinking, pressed herself against him and brushed her lips over his warm, wet flesh.

His voice was gruff. "You're doing it again. No fair taking advantage of me like that, Hollywood."

"Like what?"

"Pressing that naked body to mine. You know what it does to my willpower."

"What does it do?"

"It makes me want to do this." He turned and drew her into the circle of his arms, sending water spilling over the rim of the tub.

She giggled. "Jace, look what you're doing."

"Yeah." He shot her a grin and leaned back, dragging her on top of him. The water sloshed, spilling everywhere. But neither of them noticed as he pulled her closer—close enough for their mouths to mate.

"I know I promised you a soft bed," he murmured against her lips. "And I really intend to keep that promise. But if you don't mind—" his hands began exploring her body "—maybe we could get a head start."

She sighed as his hands moved over her. "I don't mind. But it's hard to give a back scrub when your 'client' is lying on his back."

"Yeah. You seem to have distracted me again, Hollywood."

She gasped as he took one slick nipple into his mouth...and slowly began to drive her mad.

He saw the way her eyes suddenly glazed with passion. It gave him the most erotic feeling. His hands tightened as he drew her to him until they were completely joined.

"I think we'll have to put off that bed until later. What I have in mind just can't wait."

"Neither can..."

Her words trailed off as he swept her away to paradise.

"Is that pizza I smell?" Jace climbed down from the loft and breathed in the fragrance of cheese and spices.

"I found it in the box of frozen food out in the shed." Ciara turned from the fire, where she was just removing the round tray from the hot coals. She had pulled on a turtleneck and jeans, and had left her damp hair to fall into soft curls around her face. "I hope you don't mind. I know it's not as fancy as some of the dishes you've prepared, but since our wager didn't stipulate what the loser had to fix for dinner..."

"I'm crazy about pizza. Never could get it in those

small out-of-the-way places overseas. Just smelling it makes me drool.'' He tugged on one of her curls and kissed her cheek. ''Almost as much as smelling *you* makes me drool.'' He breathed in the scent of her. ''What is that perfume you wear?''

''It's called soap and water.'' She laughed, gave his arm a shove. ''Make yourself useful. You can open that bottle of Chianti I found.''

Minutes later he was pouring red wine, while she cut the pizza and served it onto plates. Jace sipped his wine and leaned back with a sigh of contentment. ''Wine, pizza and a beautiful woman. I just don't think it gets any better.''

She studied him. He wore jeans and a fisherman's knit sweater. Beads of water glistened in his hair. He looked relaxed and content. Exactly, she realized, the way she felt. More content than at any time since she'd climbed into her car, determined to escape the media circus.

He closed a hand over hers. ''What're you smiling about, Hollywood?''

She shook her head. ''I'm just thinking what a wonderful surprise this weekend has turned out to be.''

''Yeah. For me too.''

''It should have been a disaster. An unexpected storm. No power. No way to leave.'' She turned their hands over, studying their linked fingers. ''And two very different people who were each desperate to be left alone.''

''We were, weren't we? And look at us now.''

She nodded. "Sipping wine. Eating pizza. Actually enjoying each other's company."

He shot her a meaningful look. "And looking forward to actually using a bed tonight."

She shook her head. "I should have known you'd find a way to get back to that. And I thought you were fixated on *food.*"

"That comes in a close second." He leaned over and pressed a kiss to her lips. "But my number-one fixation is you, Hollywood."

He suddenly caught her hand and dragged her to her feet. "Come on. Let's take the pizza and wine with us."

"With us? Where are we going?"

"I've just thought of a way to have it all." He winked, causing her heart to do somersaults. "We'll eat in bed."

Eleven

"Tell me about your family, Jace."

They were lying in the big bed, sipping the last of the wine, and sharing a piece of cold pizza. The bed-clothes were tangled, and they were both pleasantly sated.

"Why?"

"Because I want to know what you were like as a boy. How you grew up. What you dreamed of doing."

He shrugged, uncomfortable talking about himself. "My family started out on a hundred-thousand-acre ranch in Texas."

Ciara's eyes widened. She swallowed her pizza, then finally managed to say, "A hundred thousand acres? Jace, that's bigger than my little town, and the town next to it, and the towns on either side, and probably half the state of Kentucky all mixed to-gether."

He laughed. "Maybe not that big. But a hundred thousand acres can mean a lot of freedom for a little kid. By the time I was old enough to walk, I was riding horses. I still love to ride. But ranching wasn't for me. It appealed more to my brother, Clint."

Ciara saw his quick frown.

"Are you two close?"

He shook his head. "We never were. I was closer to my sisters—Janine, who's dead now, and Mary Ellen. But my brother Clint was a lot of things I didn't like. A bully. And a liar. I suppose that's why I deliberately chose to be as different from him as I could. So I lost myself in books, like my father."

"What did your father do?"

Jace smiled. "He was a lawyer. He wasn't much of a rancher, but he was a damn fine lawyer. I suppose he hoped one of his sons would follow him into law. But it held no interest for me."

"And so you went into journalism."

He nodded. "It's been a good life." He linked his hands under his head and stared at the ceiling. "And I've had a chance to see all those places I'd read about in books."

"Are you—" the question nearly stuck in her throat, but she forced herself to say the words "—planning on going back?"

He shrugged. "That's the sixty-four-thousand-dollar question. And I don't have an answer yet." He turned to her. "Your turn. Tell me about your brothers."

Even though she realized he'd once again smoothly changed the subject, she didn't mind. She regaled him with stories about how she'd coaxed her little brothers into acting in plays she wrote, dressing them in silly costumes she made out of cast-off paper and rags.

"We once tied my brother Michael to the clothesline and had him fly like Peter Pan. My little brother

David was Tinkerbell. You should have heard my mother when she came home and found her clothes pole broken, and the line snapped in two.''

Jace was laughing so hard, he nearly fell out of bed. ''Why didn't you ever cast yourself as the star?''

''You don't think I wanted to be hooked up to a clothesline, do you? Besides, I always had to be in charge. So I was the writer and director. That way, my poor brothers had to take orders from me.''

''Pretty smart, Hollywood.''

''Yeah, that's me. Smart.'' She set her wineglass aside and stretched out beside him. ''I wish I was smart enough to know what to do about my agent and my studio and the new contract and…things.'' She couldn't bring herself to speak of Brendan. He seemed part of another world. A world so far removed from this simple cabin that she could almost convince herself it didn't exist.

''You'll figure it out.''

She sighed. ''Or I'll make a mess of everything and have to live with it.''

''Hey.'' He leaned up on one elbow and touched his lips to hers. ''Remember what I said. You're a smart woman. You've come this far. That's no small accomplishment.''

''For a girl from the Kentucky coal-mining towns.''

''For anyone. There are plenty of actors with college degrees who wish they could be where you are in your profession. And don't you forget it. There's no reason why you can't have whatever you want out of life.''

She shook her head. ''It's funny. I suppose because I was forced to leave school at sixteen, I've always thought other people were smarter than me. Even though I read a lot, travel and meet a lot of interesting people, I've always deferred to others because of that lack of education. But I'm beginning to realize that it isn't just schooling that makes a person smart. In fact, all the education in the world can't make some people smart.''

''That's right. And remember this—from what I've read in your screenplay, you have something even better than that sharp brain of yours, Hollywood.''

''And what would that be?''

''Sensitivity. Intuition. And a real insight into people and what makes them tick.''

She squeezed his hand. ''I think I'm going to keep you around. You're very good for my ego.''

''Yeah.'' He dragged her close and kissed the top of her head. ''And if I keep on pumping up that ego, in no time at all you won't even be able to get this big head through that doorway over there.'' He lay back. ''Have you come to any decisions while you've been here?''

''Not many. At least not the important ones.'' Her lips curved into a smile. ''You know what I thought about yesterday while I was walking alone in the snow?''

''What?''

''That in my whole life, I've never had a pet. Not

a dog, or a cat, or even a goldfish. My little brother David brought home a bunny once. But that doesn't count, because my mother made him turn it loose the next day."

He stared at her. "Now that's really important."

She chuckled.

"So, Hollywood? What's your point?"

"You just said I could have whatever I want out of life. And I've decided that when I go back home I'm getting a dog. For starters, anyway. Then I may get a cat to keep him company."

"A dog. And maybe a cat." He grinned. "That's a pretty big commitment. Especially for somebody with a busy career. Remember, no matter how busy you get, a pet will depend on you for everything. Food. Shelter. Exercise, even in the rain."

She nodded. "But in return, a pet will love me. He won't care what I look like, or how much money I make, or the size of my bustline or my ego. He'll just love me. Unconditionally."

"Yeah. There's that." It was, he realized, what everyone was seeking in life. Someone, or something, to love them forever, regardless of who or what they were. Wasn't it one of the things that had been playing around the edges of his mind lately? "I think, to celebrate this momentous decision of yours, we ought to do something special."

She eyed him suspiciously. "What do you have in mind?"

He scooped her up and started out of the room.

"We've tried everything else in this cabin. I think it's time we made mad, passionate love in the loft."

Ciara awoke and lay a minute, struggling to remember where she was. A glance at the skylight told her that it was still dark, though there was the faintest smudge of dawn light tinting the inky sky.

A slow smile softened her eyes and curved her mouth as she glanced at Jace, tangled in the bed linens, asleep beside her. He was such a surprise. Smart and funny. But a dark undercurrent. He was so knowledgeable about the world. He'd been to so many places, had done so many fascinating things, had tasted so much of life. And had endured his share of sorrow. But he'd survived. And despite everything, he'd retained his sense of humor.

Best of all, he was an amazingly considerate lover. He made her feel special. He had a gift for making her believe in herself. He would never know how wonderful it was to rediscover her self-esteem. It had been at its lowest ebb when she'd first arrived at this deserted cabin. Thanks to Jace, she was almost beginning to believe that she could do whatever she set her mind to. That she could become anything she wanted.

In this man's arms, she felt safe, protected from any harm. With Jace she felt as if she'd...come home. Overcome with tenderness, she brushed the hair from his eyes and pressed her lips to his temple.

His eyes snapped open. His voice was rough with sleep. "Now what's that for?"

"For being so sweet."

"Don't say that too loudly. I'd hate to have you ruin my reputation as a tough guy."

"So that's why you resisted the bubble bath."

"Yeah. Talk about an opportunity for blackmail. I can see the headlines: War correspondent, bombing survivor Jace Lockhart drowns in bubbles."

"I wouldn't let you drown. I'd revive you with mouth-to-mouth."

He grinned. "How about some of that now?"

"Only if you're drowning."

"I am." It was true, he realized. He was awash in such confusing feelings for this woman. There was just something about her. Something sweet and vulnerable, even though he knew she was also strong and disciplined. Something that tugged at his heart, and made him want to protect her from all harm. Something so sincere about her that he was starting to believe in happy endings and forever-after.

Dangerous thoughts, he realized. But the truth was, with Ciara he had learned, too late, that she wasn't the type he could love and walk away from. The more he had, the more he wanted. Not just the pleasure she gave him. Not just the physical satisfaction. There was something deeper here. Something that was beginning to trouble him. Since that first time they'd made love, he hadn't had a single nightmare. It was as though she had somehow healed his mind and heart and soul, and driven away all his demons. With her he had found a sense of peace.

As impossible as he knew it to be, he was actually starting to think about a future with her.

He pulled her down and kissed her until they were both breathless. When they came up for air he whispered against her lips, "Thanks. I needed that." He glanced up at the skylight overhead. "It's almost morning. No point in going back to sleep. What say we try a little more mouth-to-mouth?"

"I like your ideas, Mr. Lockhart."

They were both laughing as they came together and began to kiss, but they were interrupted by a loud roaring noise in the distance. A noise that seemed to be coming closer.

Alarmed, Ciara laid a hand on Jace's arm. "What in the world is that?"

She saw his sudden frown. Her heart began to thunder. "Jace, what is it?"

His voice sounded subdued in the predawn darkness. Or was that the rough edge of frustration she heard in his tone? "If I'm not mistaken, it's the sound of snowplows."

Ciara stood beneath the skylight, watching as morning light slowly spread across the sky. Neither she nor Jace had been able to fall back to sleep.

Now, while Jace hooked up the generator in preparation for their morning shower, she peered out the frost-covered panes, wondering how far away the plows were, and how long it would take them to reach the cabin.

Who would have thought she'd feel like this? Just

days ago she believed she'd go mad at the thought of
being cooped up with a reporter in one small cabin.
And now, the very thought of having to leave Jace
was filling her with a new sort of dread.

For these few precious days she'd been in a sort of
limbo, removed from the realities of her life, and living a dream. A wonderful, romantic dream with a man
who had become a dream lover. Now it was about to
come to a screeching halt, and she would have to face
the very things that had driven her to flee in the first
place.

"All set." Jace's voice floated up to the loft. "You
should have hot water in a half hour. I'm going to
start the coffee."

"All right." She looked around at Jace's things,
still spilling out of his carryall. Her own things had
been neatly hung in the closet downstairs, or folded
into drawers. It seemed a mocking reminder of the
differences in their lives. Even though she'd only
planned on being here for a weekend, she'd had the
need for some sort of permanence. But Jace was a
rolling stone. His entire adult life had been spent living out of a suitcase. In the blink of an eye he could
be packed and off on another adventure, without a
backward glance.

This weekend would be no different. He would
leave here without giving it another thought—except
the occasional memory of a pleasant diversion. He
would return, undismayed, to his former life.

It wasn't going to be quite so easy for her. The
thought of leaving Jace was already causing a bit too

much discomfort. In fact, she couldn't bear to think about it.

She took a deep breath and pasted a smile on her face before heading down the stairs.

Jace looked up from the fire. "Let's take a walk after breakfast."

"Okay. Where to?"

"We'll climb to the top of the hill, and see if we can spot the plows."

"When do you think they'll make it here?"

He shrugged. "It could take all day. They've got a ton of snow to remove."

A day. Her heart felt lighter. As though she'd suddenly been given a reprieve.

She became aware of the fact that she was ravenous. "How about some scrambled eggs?"

"Sounds good. I'll make the toast."

As they worked together side by side, Ciara thought how easily they'd slipped into a routine. As though they'd been doing this for a lifetime.

"I found some new jelly. Wild blackberry. Try this." Jace lifted a spoon to her lips.

She tasted. Smiled. "Umm. That's great."

"I thought you'd like it. I'll set some out."

He set the table while she placed the skillet of egg mixture over the fire and began to stir.

Beside her, Jace turned the toast and gave her an admiring glance. "I've changed my mind about the French maid uniform. I think I prefer you in that football jersey."

She grinned. "I'm glad to see we're making progress. But I've been thinking that if you decide not to go back to your foreign assignments, you might want to sign on as *my* cook.''

''I might be tempted. But you'd have to tell me what my—'' he arched a brow and shot her a mock leer ''—other duties would be.''

''No more than you'd have expected of me.''

''That much, hmm? Why, Hollywood, what an evil mind you have.''

''It takes one to know one.'' She lifted the skillet from the hot coals and filled their plates. ''And there's a bonus. You wouldn't have to wear a uniform.''

''I wouldn't?''

''No.'' She sat down and picked up her fork. ''In fact, with that body of yours, I wouldn't even complain if you wore nothing at all.''

His laughter rumbled up from deep inside and spilled out in a roar. When he could find his voice he said, ''What a sexist remark, Ms. Wilde.''

''No more than I've been subjected to all my life.''

He studied her a moment before saying, ''Good point. And you're right, of course. But I hope you'll forgive the poor guys. They're just dazzled by your beauty. The same way I am.'' Before she could react to his unexpected compliment, he said, ''Let's hurry up and finish our breakfast.''

''Why?''

''The water will be hot. We can shower together, and I'll show you my…uniform. That is, if you'd care to inspect it.''

"I suppose it's the least I can do, before considering your employment."

They were still exchanging teasing barbs as they lingered over their breakfast, then washed the dishes and headed toward the shower.

An hour later they were pulling on their parkas. Jace rummaged in the closet for their skis. "As long as we're going to hike all the way to the top of the hill, we may as well take the easy way down."

"Good idea." Ciara stepped outside, shouldering her skis.

The air carried the sweet scent of spring, and was made even warmer by the bright sunshine. As they trudged through the snow, they could feel the steady drip from the trees overhead.

Jace nodded toward the rushing stream, swollen with runoff from the melting snow. "In a matter of days there won't even be a trace of this snowstorm."

His words caused a sudden ache in her heart. Wasn't it true of them, as well? Didn't it stand to reason that once they returned to their careers, this time spent together would vanish without a trace?

Well, that might be true for Jace. For herself, she thought fiercely, she would never forget this weekend. Or the man who had made it so special.

They climbed to the top of the hill and gazed around. Though the surrounding countryside was still cloaked in white, there were occasional patches of brown. Many of the evergreens had shaken off their mantle of snow. The crisscrossed tracks left by birds and animals attested to the fact that the storm had given up its hold on nature.

Jace stared around, then touched a hand to Ciara's shoulder and pointed. "There are the plows. See?"

She caught sight of them, inching along the main highway. She nodded, feeling a mixture of relief and dismay. Relief because it would surely take them the rest of the day to reach the cabin. Dismay because there would be no holding them back now. Once the roads were cleared, she would have no reason to remain.

She glanced at Jace and realized that he was probably struggling with the same thoughts. "Come on." She clamped on her skis. "It'll be slow going in this wet snow. But I still intend to race you down."

He caught her arm. "Wait a minute. You forgot to mention the prize."

"Did I?" She shot him a challenging smile. "You owe me a back scrub. And I intend to win it."

Jace watched her shove off. For an instant he thought about holding back, and allowing her to win. Then just as quickly he dismissed the idea. He'd always known only one way to play, and that was to win. If Ciara wanted that back scrub badly enough, she'd damn well have to be good enough to earn it.

He shoved off, too, and caught up with her at the line of trees. By the time he veered to the left, he was half a length ahead. When he emerged on the other side of the trees, he heard the sound of her laughter, and caught sight of a flash as she sped past him. Her laughter trailed on the breeze.

Even as he was forced to bend down into a crouch, hoping to turn on some speed, he had to admire her style. It would appear that Ciara Wilde was no slouch when it came to winning either.

Maybe that was one more reason he ought to put aside this uneasiness he'd been feeling all morning, and just be glad the plows had finally made it through. Because the truth was, he was beginning to care way too much about this woman. And that knowledge made him extremely uncomfortable. After all, what was he going to do? Marry her?

He waited for the resistance that always pushed its way to the forefront of his mind whenever he thought about settling down. But this time it didn't come. Instead, he found himself enjoying the image of Ciara as his wife. And maybe even…a baby. Or two.

He was so deep in thought that he never even saw the half-buried log in the snow until his skis hit it, sending him flying through the air. He landed in a snowbank, facedown.

By the time he'd located his skis and started back down the hill, he could see Ciara already going into the last turn before reaching the cabin. She was little more than a blur of color against the snow.

He muttered a halfhearted curse. That would teach him to stop daydreaming when he ought to have his mind on more important things.

Then he grinned. The truth was, he was just as happy to be the loser this time. He was really looking forward to scrubbing her back. And other things.

Twelve

Ciara lay in the big bed beside Jace, watching the steady rise and fall of his chest as he slept. He'd been restless through the night. Restless and pacing. And though he hadn't complained, she surmised that it was the pain in his leg that had him walking the floor. The spill he'd taken while skiing had no doubt aggravated his injury. Just before dawn she'd seen him swallow a pill. Now, finally, he had found some peace, though he'd tossed aside the blankets in a fit of discomfort.

She studied the scar that ran from his hip to his ankle. The pain from such a wound would be bad enough to endure. But what sort of anguish must he have suffered, wondering whether or not he would lose his leg? For a man like Jace Lockhart—a fiercely independent, well-respected journalist who prided himself on his ability to go anywhere necessary to cover the news of the world—it must have been a terrifying experience. And yet he'd found the courage within himself to fight his way back to health.

There was such strength in him. Not only physical strength, but a strength of will that touched a chord in her. They were so different, and yet—in many ways—so alike. Each of them had displayed a single-minded purpose as they had pursued their goals. Each of them had overcome many obstacles. Yet, amid the rubble of their past, they were still standing.

She felt a sense of fierce pride in that fact. A town like Hollywood could eat people alive. Yet, despite her lack of formal education and the many detours she'd been forced to take in her career, she was still working. Oh, her head might often be in the clouds, harboring all kinds of future dreams, but she was able to keep her feet firmly planted on the ground.

She lifted her head, listening intently. She could hear the return of the plows in the distance. The sound of their engines had filled the night air, continuing on until almost midnight. And now, although it was barely light, they were already back at work, clearing the mountain roads. Why did they have to be so damnably efficient? The irony of her conflicting feelings made her grit her teeth. Just days ago she would have rejoiced if she could have been spared the company of this man. And now, thanks to the hardworking road crews, she'd just lost her best excuse for staying with him.

She pressed a hand to the little throbbing that was beginning at her temple. She shouldn't think so much, she told herself.

As she started to ease herself from bed, strong fingers closed around her wrist, holding her still. "Jace." She glanced at his face and found him staring at her with a strange, intense look. "I was trying not to bother you."

"Impossible, Hollywood. You've been bothering

me from the moment I met you. And what a meeting. At the end of a rifle.''

She gave an embarrassed laugh. ''What else could I do? You had me scared half to death.''

''Really?'' He lifted a hand to brush the hair from her eyes. ''And I thought you looked cool enough to nail my hide to the wall.''

''That would have been a pity.'' She trailed a finger across his chest, and saw his eyes narrow fractionally. ''It's such a lovely hide.''

''Yours isn't half-bad either. Especially that first glimpse you gave me. Come to think of it, I haven't seen that sexy little thong since. What happened to it?''

''I was mortified to be caught in that. I was just undressing when I heard the approach of a car. I was so terrified that I'd been found out by a news crew, that I wasn't even thinking straight. There wasn't time to do more than grab that rifle and switch off the lights. The next thing I knew, I was being roughed-up by a stranger. You know something, Jace? You'll never know how scared I was. I really thought you might be some sort of escaped rapist or killer, until you said the name Fortune. Then I was just humiliated.''

''Then you're one hell of a good actress, Hollywood. All I saw was this hissing, spitting she-cat who wanted to scratch out my eyes.''

''That probably would have worked better than the rifle. I don't really know how to fire one of them.''

''It shows. You forgot to take off the safety.''

Her eyes widened. "You mean you knew I couldn't shoot you?"

"Not right away. When I felt the press of a rifle in my ribs in the darkness, I knew only one thing—survival. But later, when I switched on the lights, I realized you wouldn't have been able to do much more than knock me over the head with it. But by then, I was so dazzled by the sight of you in that...almost invisible underwear, you had a distinct advantage over me. A good thing you didn't realize it, or this whole weekend might have ended before it began."

"*Now* you tell me." Ciara was laughing as she swung her feet to the floor.

Jace's fingers tightened on her wrist. His lips curved in a lazy, knowing smile. "Stay in bed awhile."

"I'm not sure I should. You know what that always leads to."

"Yeah." He hauled her into his arms and covered her mouth with his. "I'm counting on it."

As soon as Ciara opened the cabin door and stepped onto the porch she became acutely aware of the change in the weather. The warm southern breeze was positively balmy. Water dripped from the roof and ran in rivulets, melting the snow around the steps. A chorus of birds sang in the nearby trees. A rabbit nibbling grass beneath the shelter of a towering pine scampered away as Ciara stepped off the porch and headed toward the shed.

The snow had already disappeared from the roof of the shed, and the path leading to it was a river of water. But instead of lifting her spirits, the return of spring had the opposite effect on her. She felt a overwhelming sadness at the sight of the melting snow.

A short time later she returned to the cabin, carrying the fixings for a breakfast of eggs, sausage and pancakes. As she entered she called, "It's a good thing we got in our skiing when we did."

Jace looked up from the fire, where he was adding another log. "Why is that?"

She nodded toward the window. "The snow's melting so quickly, the hillsides will be bare in places by this time tomorrow." She turned away and busied herself in the kitchen, trying not to think of the implications. But the truth was there, lying like a stone around her heart as she crossed to the fireplace, scrambling eggs and turning sausage in a skillet. The snow was melting. The plows were on the move. In no time, she would be free to leave.

Free to leave. What a strange expression. She poured pancake batter into a skillet, then sat back on her heels, deep in thought. If she were truly free, she would never leave this place. Or this man. She'd found something rare and wonderful here in this cabin, in Jace's arms. She wished, with all her being, that she could simply hide away here with him and never return to the life she'd known. But she wasn't free. She had duties, obligations. And no matter how much she wished otherwise, she would have to go back and face them.

Then there was Jace. He had obligations of his own. A man like Jace Lockhart would never be willing to give up the excitement of his world travels and settle down into a routine.

"Hey, Hollywood." Jace pulled the skillet from the fire before the pancakes could burn. "Where's your mind?"

"Oh. Sorry." Avoiding his eyes, she filled a platter, then took a seat beside him.

Jace tasted, sighed with pleasure. "I bet I've gained ten pounds since I got here."

She gave him an admiring glance. "You don't have an ounce of fat anywhere on that body."

He arched a brow. "You've been peeking, haven't you?"

"More than peeking." She sipped her coffee and studied him over the rim of her cup. "As a matter of fact, I've looked you over very carefully. And I declare you one fine specimen."

"Now, coming from one of the world's most beautiful women, I take that as a high compliment indeed."

"'World's most beautiful women.'" She gave a snort of disgust.

"As I recall, you topped a magazine's list of the world's most beautiful people last year. They had a full-length shot of you on their cover. And I spent many a night drooling over it."

"You did?" She lifted her nose in the air. "You really need to get a life. Besides," she added, "that was last year. This year I'll probably be replaced by a sixteen-year-old nymph, and the magazine staff won't even remember how to spell my name.''

''Cynic.'' He helped himself to another pancake and liberally poured syrup over it.

''Maybe. But if I've learned anything it's that the public is fickle. Especially when it comes to actors who start to believe their own publicity.''

''No chance of that happening to you, Hollywood. You're your own worst critic.'' He caught her by the chin and kissed her, hard and quick. ''Come on. Indulge yourself. We won't count the calories. We'll just enjoy the moment.''

How could she argue, when he was so persuasive? She slid a pancake onto her plate and followed his lead, slathering it with syrup. As she took the first bite she muttered, ''I'm going to need a really tough workout right after breakfast, if I'm going to overcome all these fat grams.''

He lifted her hand to his lips. ''Hollywood, I have the perfect exercise in mind.''

She closed her eyes and pretended to groan, before bursting into gales of laughter. ''Now why did I know you'd make just such an offer?''

''Because that's the kind of guy I am. Always willing to sacrifice myself for the sake of a damsel in distress.''

Even while she laughed with him, Ciara realized that Jace had deliberately kept the conversation light for her sake. It was one more reason to love him.

And I do love him, she thought. Though it didn't seem possible to be responding this way to someone she'd known such a short time, there was no denying what she felt for this man. It was stronger, deeper, than anything she'd ever felt about any man. Even Brendan.

The thought left her breathless, and more than a little sad. Because the truth was, the timing was all wrong. The timing and the circumstances. Neither she nor Jace had the time to give this relationship what it needed to develop into something lasting and permanent.

A short time later, as they were putting away the last of the clean dishes, the lights in the cabin flickered, then came on. There was an unexpected humming in the room—the sound of the refrigerator.

They stared at one another in surprise. Then Jace opened the refrigerator door and saw the interior light come on.

"Well." Ciara struggled to keep her tone even. "Looks like the power's on. I guess we can haul the food back from the shed now."

"Yeah." He caught sight of her little frown, and quipped, "you did say you wanted to work off your breakfast, didn't you?"

She nodded and, following his lead, pulled on her parka. "I think I like your first idea better."

He draped an arm around her shoulders as they trudged through the snow to the shed. "Right after this, we'll try my way. I promise it'll be much more pleasant than hauling in food. And just think," he muttered against her temple, "We can even enjoy a hot shower together afterward."

She brightened. "I'm beginning to like your idea even more. Come on. Let's get this little chore over with."

They made several trips from the shed to the cabin, returning the food to the refrigerator. Just as they finished, they heard the roar of the plow as it moved up the steep path and came to a halt at the door of the cabin.

Jace stepped onto the porch and waved to the driver, then walked over to the truck, while Ciara remained in the doorway, watching and listening.

"How're the main roads?" Jace shouted as the driver rolled down his window.

"Most of them are clear. There are still a few patches of snow and ice. But by morning you folks should have no problem getting out of here."

Morning. Ciara's heart dropped.

"I bet you two can't wait to get back to civilization," the driver shouted over the roar of his engine.

"Yeah." Jace's voice lacked conviction.

"Would you like some coffee before you leave?" Ciara called to him.

"No, thanks." The driver held up an insulated mug. "Brought my own. But I appreciate the offer. I'll be going now. I still have a lot of work ahead of me. Oh!" he called as an afterthought. "I don't suppose you folks have a problem being interviewed."

"Interviewed?" Jace frowned. "What are you talking about?"

"I spotted a couple of those television news vans out on the highway waiting until I plowed this lane.

I figure as soon as it's clear, they'll want to interview
people like you who've been stuck in this snowstorm
for the past couple of days. How about that? You'll
get to see yourselves on TV.''

With a wave he backed the truck down the lane,
executed a turn, and was gone.

In the silence that followed, Jace made up his mind
quickly. As he began a sweep of the cabin he said
calmly, ''Better grab a parka and some boots, Hollywood, and hide back in the shed.''

''Hide? But—''

''No time to argue. Just do as I say.'' He headed
for the bedroom, drawing draperies on all the windows as he went.

Ciara pulled on her boots and snatched up her
parka. Without taking time to slip it on, she ran from
the cabin and yanked open the door to the shed. Just
as she stepped inside, she could hear the sound of
vehicles approaching. She crouched behind the shed
door, listened to the slamming of doors and the sound
of voices. Though she couldn't see, she strained to
make out the words.

''Hey.'' A reporter with carefully sprayed hair,
wearing a parka over his suit and tie, stepped from
the news van and started toward the porch. Behind
him walked a bearded photographer, aiming his video
camera at the cabin. A second news truck pulled up
and several more men and women spilled out. They
quickly began to fan out, moving around the cabin,
focusing their cameras on the door and on every window.

Jace opened the door and stood facing them. "What brings you up here?"

"We don't want to bother anybody," the handsome reporter called in his friendliest voice. "We're looking for Ciara Wilde. Know her?"

Jace smiled. "Are you talking about the actress?"

"Know any other Ciara Wilde?"

Though he was inwardly seething, Jace managed to show no emotion. "What would a gorgeous movie star be doing in the middle of nowhere?"

"Hiding out, maybe. She's missing."

"Then what makes you think she's hiding out? Maybe she's been kidnapped."

The news crew glanced at one another nervously. "Could be." The reporter seemed to be mulling it over. "Our theory is that she just wants the publicity. At any rate, our magazine is paying a hefty bounty for the first pictures of her."

"A bounty, huh? You make it sound like the Wild West. Just how much is her hide fetching these days?"

"Quarter of a million."

"Half a million," a second reporter corrected. She had short lacquered red hair, and was wearing a red coat with a white scarf at the throat. The second reporter moved closer. "We'd be willing to share, of course, if someone were to show us where she is."

"That's a lot of money." Jace dug a hand in his pocket, and came up with a handful of crumpled bills. "As you can see, I could use some. But..." He shrugged. "I'm sorry to say I'm all alone at the moment."

The reporter started up on the porch. "Mind if we look around?"

Jace's eyes narrowed. "Yeah. I'd mind a lot."

At the look in his eyes she backed up a step, moving so quickly that the photographer filming behind her had to duck to one side to avoid being bumped.

The first reporter was studying Jace with great interest. "You look familiar. Don't I know you?"

Jace lifted a brow. "You might have seen me on TV. I've been covering the war in Eastern Europe for the past few years."

"A correspondent?"

"That's right. I'm here on vacation."

"Some vacation." The two reporters glanced at each other, then at Jace. "You picked a hell of a time to come to the mountains."

"Yeah." Jace managed a smile. "Pretty boring. No phone. No electricity. But at least I got plenty of rest."

The first reporter stuck out his hand. "Look, we're really sorry we bothered you. We had a tip that Ciara Wilde was friends with the owners of this place. It was just a wild-goose chase, but we have to follow every lead. You understand."

Jace nodded. "Yeah. I've followed plenty of leads myself."

He remained on the porch, watching as the reporters and photographers returned to their vehicles. As they drove away he carefully locked the cabin door, then, with a look of fury, made his way to the shed.

When he yanked open the door, he saw Ciara cringe and turn away from the sunlight, as though it were the lights of dozens of cameras. He stood a moment regarding her. "So. That's the price you pay for being a movie star. What are they after?"

She paused a moment, realizing that this was the perfect opportunity to tell him everything about herself and her reason for hiding away this weekend. A part of her actually looked forward to the cleansing that would come with a full confession. But another part of her recoiled at the thought of baring her soul. They had so little time left together. Why spoil even a minute of it with talk of a part of her life that didn't involve Jace? Her engagement to Brendan was already over, at least in her own mind. Why drag it out for discussion now?

As the silence stretched out between them, she knew that the time for the truth had passed.

He was staring at her with such intensity, she had to look away. "Are you saying this happens all the time, Hollywood?"

She drew a ragged breath. "Often enough that I hate going out in public."

Jace felt a wave of fierce protectiveness. He was beginning to understand just what Ciara had been enduring.

"These people call themselves reporters?" What they really were, he thought angrily, were bounty hunters. They were going after her as though she were a hardened criminal. And the only crime Ciara had committed was to be beautiful and famous. That made her fodder for every magazine and tabloid that made its profit by stalking celebrities.

He glanced at a toboggan standing in a corner of the shed. He walked over and hauled it down, then caught her hand.

"What do you think you're doing?" she demanded.

"Taking you out for some fun, Hollywood. Come on. I know just what you need to put these people out of your mind once and for all."

Thirteen

Jace kept Ciara's hand in his as they climbed the steep hill behind the cabin. For the first half of the climb, neither of them spoke. Jace kept a tight rein on his anger, knowing that if he said a single word, it would come spilling out. Instead, he let the magic of the day weave its spell. The sunlight reflecting off the snow was so blinding that it almost hurt. But there was no longer any bite to the breeze. Instead, it felt wonderfully clean and inviting.

By the time they reached the halfway mark, Jace's anger had begun to evaporate. He glanced over at Ciara, and realized that her fear was slipping away as well. Hell, he thought, they'd both been trying to hold it all together while their little fantasy was falling apart around them. It was time to let it all go—and just relax.

"How long has it been since you were on a toboggan?"

She shrugged. "I've never been on one."

"What?" He stopped and turned to her. "Are you telling me you've missed one of my most cherished childhood memories? Didn't you get enough snow in Kentucky?"

"Sure. We got plenty of snow. But we never owned a toboggan."

"How did you manage to slide down hills?"

"We used the lids off garbage pails. They made great sleds."

"Well, a toboggan is even better. You're in for a rare treat." He caught her hand. "Come on. Let's get moving."

When they finally reached the top of the hill, they paused to catch their breath.

"Oh. Look, Jace." Ciara pointed to the highway far below. It ran like a darkened ribbon through the blanket of white.

"Pretty impressive."

"So are you." She tucked her arm in his. "I didn't know how you'd get rid of those news crews. I guess I figured you sent me to the shed so I wouldn't hear you threatening them, or see you beating them mercilessly."

"Well, I did neither. Why are you impressed?"

"Because you got rid of them so smoothly. A few words, and they just calmly got in their vans and rode away. That never happens when I'm around."

"That's why I sent you to the shed. I figured if they were any good at their business at all, they'd surround the cabin and aim those telephoto lenses through the windows, looking for some sign of you."

"What makes you think they won't come back?"

He sent her one of his heart-stopping grins. "Oh, they'll be back. In fact, I figure right about now, they're sniffing around the cabin, trying to peek inside."

Her eyes got as big as saucers. "Then, what are we doing up here?"

"Getting out of their way so they can satisfy their curiosity."

"But, Jace, what if they see something of mine?"

"I drew all the draperies. I locked the door. And the shed has no window. They can't see your car inside."

She took a deep breath, considering. "You think that'll be enough to satisfy them?"

"It better be." Though he tried to keep his tone light, there was an edge of steel beneath it, leaving her no doubt that he'd do whatever it took to protect her. "Now come on. We're going to forget everything except playing in the snow."

"I like the sound of that."

He laughed. "I wish I'd known that earlier. There are all kinds of ways to play in the snow."

"I'll settle for the toboggan right now."

"Okay." He leaned close. "Your way first. Then my way later."

He hauled the toboggan to the very edge of the hill before he helped Ciara to sit down, showing her how to tuck her feet in front of her. Then he gave the toboggan a shove and leapt on, settling himself behind her. The wind whistled past their faces and they gathered speed until they felt as though they were flying.

Ciara leaned back in Jace's arms and let out a scream of delight.

He pressed his mouth to her ear. "What did I tell you? Isn't this fantastic?"

"I love it."

Just then he shouted, "Okay! Lean to the left."

She did as he said and the toboggan veered slightly, missing a cluster of trees and skimming lightly over the snowdrifts. Familiar landmarks, a fallen tree, a half-buried boulder, flew by.

By the time they reached the bottom of the hill, they were laughing and gasping for breath. They rolled to a stop, and Jace helped her up. "Want to go again?"

"Oh, yes." Her eyes were shining with excitement. Her cheeks were bright red. Her hair was windswept and tousled.

Jace thought she'd never looked lovelier. "Okay, Hollywood." He pulled her close and gave her a hard, quick kiss. Then he gathered the pull-rope and caught her hand in his. "Time to climb the mountain again."

"I can't wait." She danced along beside him, oblivious to the drifts that made walking an effort. "What other things did you do as a kid?"

"I had a sled. And a pair of snowshoes. But mostly I rode horses. Summer and winter. And by the time I was a teen, I was into parasailing, and learning to fly a plane, and—"

She stopped him with a hand to his lips. "Wait a minute. Back up. You can fly a plane?"

He gave her a mock look of surprise. "Can't everyone?"

"Are you serious?"

He laughed. "It was just something I'd always wanted to do. So I got a part-time job after school and saved enough for lessons."

"Do you own your own plane?"

He shook his head. "I toyed with the idea when I was in college. Too expensive. Not only to buy, but to maintain. And then, once I left the country, I gave up the idea. Too many licenses in too many little countries. Not to mention all those guns going off. I may be pretty fearless, but I don't harbor a death wish."

Ciara shot him a sideways glance. "And you parasail?"

"You don't?"

"Jace." She tugged on his arm. "I'm serious. You can fly and parasail? When did you find the time to do all these things?"

"Those were in my younger days, when I wasn't driven to work twenty-four hours a day. Didn't you ever just do fun, foolish things to amuse yourself?"

She shook her head. "I never had the time. I was always working twenty-four hours a day."

"See, Hollywood. That's what's wrong with you," he teased. "You don't know how to relax and have fun."

They were at the top of the hill again, and Ciara settled herself into the front of the toboggan. "You're right!" she called over her shoulder as Jace shoved them both off again. "But I'm a really fast learner. So brace yourself, Jace. I might make you climb this mountain a dozen times before I've had enough."

"I think every muscle in my body aches," Jace muttered as he hauled the toboggan over a series of snowdrifts toward the shed.

"Do I hear you complaining?" Ciara caught his arm and pressed a kiss to his cheek. "Isn't this the man who boasted that he just wanted to have fun?"

"Fun is sliding down the hill half a dozen times. Anything over that is work. And after fifteen times, it's definitely considered punishment."

"I had the time of my life."

"Yeah. I could tell. You made enough noise for a whole playground of kids."

"Well, since I never got to do this as a girl, I had to make up for lost time."

When he had finished stowing the toboggan, Ciara caught his hands. "Thank you, Jace." She brushed a kiss over his lips. "I can't remember when I've had such fun."

When she started to pull away he drew her back and rubbed his lips over hers. "Hey, now I remember why I love showing you a good time. You have the nicest way of showing your gratitude."

She wrapped her arms around his neck. "Maybe that's because you're so receptive."

"Yeah. Well, I'd hate to have you believing that your effort was wasted." He lifted his hands to frame her face. "Go ahead. Thank me all you want."

She leaned into him, allowing the kiss to slowly deepen, while her hands slipped under his parka. "I really, really loved this afternoon, Jace."

He nibbled her lower lip. "I'm glad. So did I."

He could feel the heat beginning to spread. Just minutes ago he'd been chilled from the snow. Now he wanted nothing more than to slip off his heavy coat and take her, right here in the shed, with the fragrance of evergreen surrounding them.

"If you're not careful, Hollywood, we might not be able to make it to the warm cabin."

"I don't mind if *you* don't."

He paused a moment to draw back and study her. Seeing that she was serious, he unzipped her parka and unbuttoned her flannel shirt, all the while staring deeply into her eyes.

She did the same, opening his parka, then tugging his shirt from the waistband so that she could feel the warm, firm flesh of his back against her palms.

His mouth fused with hers in a kiss so hot, so hungry, it left her gasping. His hands moved over her, weaving a magic of their own, until she could feel her blood heating, her head spinning in dizzying circles.

Before she could recover, he backed her against the wall, then lifted her, until her legs were wrapped around his waist.

"Jace." His name was torn from her lips, and then the breath backed up in her lungs. Everything sped up. Her pulse rate thundered. When she could breathe again, it was to moan with pleasure, to pant from between parted lips.

She wrapped herself around him, feeling like a volcano about to erupt. All seething steam and molten lava, moving faster and faster toward the surface until, without warning, she exploded at the same time he did, in a sea of bright color and unbearable heat.

Dazed, she clung weakly to him, knowing if he let go of her, she would slump, weak and boneless, to the floor.

He kept his hands at her shoulders, pressing her firmly against the length of him while he kissed her, long and slow and deep. Against her mouth he muttered, "I think you're going to be the death of me, Hollywood. But at least I'll die a happy man."

Before returning to the cabin, they walked in a slow circle around the exterior. Just as Jace had suspected, there were dozens of footprints, especially near the door and windows. Fortunately, it was impossible to see past the heavy draperies that covered the windows.

"Looks like our news crews left empty-handed."

"Do you think they'll come back?"

He shook his head. "How much time can they waste following a dead trail? They've probably got a hundred more leads to check out. Come on. I think it's safe to say you're home-free."

He unlocked the door, and they stepped inside. The fire had burned to coals, and Jace tossed several logs

on the hearth before slipping out of his parka and
boots.

He filled the kettle with water and placed it on a
burner. "This should be a novelty," he said with a
laugh. "We can actually use the stove." He turned.
"That reminds me." He crossed the room and picked
up the phone. Hearing a dial tone he said, "The phone
line's working. People must be worried about you—
you're free to call them."

Ciara thought about Brendan, and wondered briefly
how he'd been handling her absence. How he was
explaining it to friends, and especially to the media.
Knowing Brendan, he'd have come up with a plau-
sible story. As for what she would tell him... She
realized she couldn't possibly discuss any of this in
a phone call. She'd wait until she could do it face-to-
face.

Then there were Eden and Emily. She owed it to
her friends to let them know that the weekend at the
cabin had been all she'd hoped for. And so much
more. When she thought about the lunch with the two
women, just over a month ago, she smiled. At the
time, she'd been so tired, so confused about her engagement, her career. When Eden had offered her this
sanctuary, a safe and private place to go to sort out
her troubles, it seemed she might finally be able to
think about the future without feeling hysteria well up
inside her. It didn't seem possible that she was now
calm and centered and resigned to so many changes
in her life.

But that admission would have to come later—

when she was alone and settled back in her own home. Then she would reassure Eden and Emily that this weekend had been the finest gift a friend could give another.

She shook her head. "I don't have any calls to make. Help yourself to the phone."

Jace looked at her a little suspiciously, but climbed to the loft and returned with his laptop computer, plugging the modem into the phone line. "I think it's time I checked my e-mail."

As he scanned his computer screen, he nodded. "Just as I thought. Brad has sent me dozens of e-mails, wondering where the hell I am and why I'm not answering him." He glanced up and, seeing her questioning look, explained, "Brad Thompson is the one I told you about—the director of overseas news at the network. He's also a good friend. It was Brad who suggested I take a leave of absence until I decide what I want to do with the rest of my life." He bent to the keyboard and began typing.

For several minutes Ciara watched him. Then, feeling melancholy, she made her way to the bedroom, closing the door behind her. She picked up her screenplay and walked to the chair, determined to keep her mind occupied. But it was impossible. As soon as she sat down she found herself staring out the window.

Jace's words kept coming back to taunt her. ... *what I want to do with the rest of my life.*

She felt the way she had when she was that frightened little girl in Kentucky. Always wishing and wanting and dreaming. And feeling trapped in a situation beyond her control.

She knew that their little idyll had just ended. She had to face the fact that she had no more excuses. No matter how badly she wanted to remain here, hidden away, she had no choice but to leave in the morning, and go back to the life she'd fled. There were decisions to be made that would affect her future. And she was the only one capable of making them.

As for Jace, he was already communicating with his co-workers, and preparing to deal with his own future. A future that, no matter how hard she wished otherwise, couldn't possibly include her.

Through sheer force of will, Ciara managed to work on her screenplay for several hours. The mental exercise was good for her. She saw it as a test—one she passed with flying colors. She was relieved that she could still summon the discipline needed to complete a task when it was absolutely necessary. Her heart might not be in it, but she could force herself to concentrate.

When she emerged from her room, Jace was just entering the cabin with an armload of logs. The weather outside had warmed so much that he hadn't even bothered to wear his parka. She watched as he piled the logs neatly beside the hearth, then went to work building a fire. Her throat went dry at the ripple of muscle beneath the rolled sleeves of his shirt. She loved the feel of those strong, muscled arms holding her. Loved the press of his hard body against hers. She found the intensity in his eyes deeply erotic. As was the teasing laughter in his voice, which she'd found so unexpected. Her first glimpse of him had led her to think he was a harsh, bitter man. It had been such a delight to discover those quick flashes of humor. He was a rare combination. A man so easy on the eye that he was bound to turn women's heads, yet didn't care about his looks. A natural athlete, who had chosen to develop his mind as well as his body. And a reporter who, perhaps because of his years reporting on the horrors of war, had a strong social conscience. And a man who, despite his attempts to appear tough, had a truly kind heart. There was no denying that she loved everything about him.

He straightened, turned. Seeing the look in her eyes, he walked to her without a word and gathered her into his arms.

"I missed you." He spoke the words against a tangle of hair at her temple.

"I was just in the next room. You could have knocked."

"Uh-uh. I'd have been intruding on your business. And I'd never want to do that. I figured you were working on your screenplay, and I know it's important to you."

"It is. But so are you."

"Thanks." He brushed his lips across her forehead. "I kept wishing you'd come out here with me."

"I didn't want to intrude on *your* business. You looked like you were enjoying all those messages on your e-mail."

"I was. But not nearly as much as I enjoy you."

He kissed her lips and felt the familiar rush of heat. His fingers tightened at her shoulders. "What would you like for dinner?"

"I'm not hungry." The thought of food suddenly repulsed her.

"Me neither. I couldn't even look at food right now."

"Jace." She took a step back, determined to say this as calmly as possible. "You know that I have to leave in the morning. It's not that I want to, but I really have to."

He shook his head. "We won't talk about that now."

"We don't have to talk about it, but I think it's important that we both face facts."

"We'll face them later."

"But that won't change any—" He scooped her up into his arms and started toward the bedroom. "Jace, what are you doing?"

"You said you're not hungry. I'm not hungry. So I thought we'd skip dinner and go directly to dessert."

She was laughing as he carried her through the doorway and deposited her on her feet. "This won't solve anything."

"Want to bet?"

"Jace. You're just putting off the—"

He cut off her protest with a kiss. And then, as his lips moved over hers, she forgot everything except the taste of him, and the wonderful feel of those big hands moving over her, and the slow, simmering heat building deep inside.

She knew that morning would come far too soon. And with it, all the unpleasant facts they were both dreading. Facts that would erase, in the blink of an eye, this fairy-tale fantasy they had created.

But that was tomorrow. For now, she would pretend that tomorrow would never come. They were just two lovers who had all the time in the world. To hold each other. To love each other. To soothe each other's hurts. For now, she would lose herself in the pleasure he was offering.

Together, they would hold back, for as long as possible, the pain of separation.

"You're sure you have to leave?" Sometime before dawn, Jace pressed his mouth to Ciara's temple and lingered there, loving the feel of her skin against his lips.

They'd hardly slept. The realization that it was their last night together had added a raw, desperate edge to their lovemaking. And so they'd come together in a storm of passion that had staggered both of them. Even when they managed to doze, they awoke to a new, sharper hunger, which only added another layer to their passion.

She propped herself on one elbow to look into his eyes. "I have to go back, Jace. There are…things I have to attend to." She struggled to put on a brave face. "But just think. Now you'll have the solitude you were hoping for."

"Yeah." There was a hint of pain in that word, and for a moment he fell silent. Then he seemed to pull himself back from the edge of his dark thoughts.

He twirled a strand of her hair around his finger, watching the way the morning sunlight turned the ends to gold. "So, do you think if I tried a little more...persuasion, I could change your mind?"

She felt the quick stuttering of her heart as he drew her down and brushed soft, seductive little kisses over her eyes, her cheeks, the tip of her nose. "I don't know about changing my mind. But it would certainly send me on my way with a satisfied smile."

"You know something, Hollywood? You're a greedy woman." He plunged his hands into her hair and covered her mouth with his.

She was staggered by the love she felt for him at this moment. "And you're a very generous man, Jace Lockhart, sacrificing yourself like this."

"Damn right I am." Swamped with emotions himself, he proceeded to show her all the love, all the passion, all the desire he was feeling. The love he felt for this woman in his arms left him shattered.

And then there was no need for words as they slipped into a world reserved for lovers. A world of soft sighs and gentle touches. A world of kisses and caresses. A world filled with touch and taste and feelings so overpowering, so deeply moving, they were both overwhelmed.

Fourteen

"Jace." Ciara looked up from the bag she was packing. "Where are you going?"

He jingled his keys. "I thought I'd drive to the nearest town. Pick up some supplies. It'll give me a chance to see how clear the roads are. I don't trust that toy you call a car."

She folded a sweatshirt, set it aside. "You're just looking for an excuse to keep me here another day."

"You got that right." With a grin he pulled her close and kissed her. "Think it'll work?"

Oh, if only he knew how desperately she wanted to stay. But she managed a smile. "Not a chance. But I admire your persistence. How long will you be gone?"

He shrugged. "No more than an hour or two. I'll just gas the Jeep and pick up some groceries. And maybe check out a little chapel I saw on the way up here the night of the storm."

"A chapel?"

"Yeah. Just a little country church. I noticed it because I was afraid at the time that I might have to take shelter there. Now I've been thinking it would make a great wedding chapel."

She was afraid to breathe. Afraid that if he knew

how those words made her reel inwardly, he'd realize just how hard she'd fallen. So she asked casually, "Is somebody you know planning a wedding?"

Was that fear he heard in her voice? Had she actually backed away a step or two? Not that he blamed her. He couldn't believe he'd actually blurted out such a thing. But now that he had, he had to cover his lapse. What had he been thinking? It was too soon to let her know what he was feeling. He had no right to stand in the way of her career. Especially in light of the problems she needed to deal with. Whatever he wanted from this relationship, he would have to be patient, and wait until she'd resolved her own problems first. Then, they could move on to something more...permanent.

He merely smiled. "Don't worry, Hollywood. I won't be long."

Disappointed at his response, she let out the breath she'd been holding, and tried to ignore the little twinge in her heart. As always, her overactive imagination had conjured something that wasn't even there. She cursed her foolishness. The last thing Jace Lockhart would be thinking about was anything that would tie him down. After all, covering wars in foreign countries was hardly the sort of life-style that would permit thoughts of marriage. "I'll be packed and ready by the time you get back."

That's what he was afraid of. He sauntered out the door, hoping against hope for a miracle. Like totally impassable roads. Or another freak snowstorm. But a glance at the sky assured him of the worst. It was a clear, cloudless day, with sunshine so bright it hurt his eyes. That meant only one thing: nature wasn't going to give him any help. This time, he was on his own.

On the long ride to town he reminded himself that he'd always been an impulsive man. He'd gone to countries most people had never even heard of. Had taken assignments that sane journalists would run from. But this time he might just be doing the most impulsive thing he'd ever done. He was actually considering asking Ciara to stay in his life forever.

He felt a little like a man leaping off a cliff. Exhilarated. Light-headed. And scared to death.

In Jace's absence Ciara took a slow stroll around the cabin, determined to store up every memory. She stood in front of the fireplace, remembering the way she'd felt when Jace had first unleashed that hidden passion. She closed her eyes a moment, amazed at the feelings that pulsed through her even now. She could actually feel the dizzying fear she'd experienced, as if she'd been on a roller coaster. He'd taken her higher than she'd ever been. With Jace, the ride had been breathless.

She climbed the loft and sat on the edge of the bed, tilting her head up to stare at the sunlight spilling down through the skylight. Despite the warmth of the sun, she shivered, remembering the sound of the snowplows—the end of their fantasy.

Downstairs once more she stood deep in thought alongside the hot tub, remembering so many things.

Jace's unexpected gift of a warm bath after her long trek in the snow. It had lifted her spirits as nothing else could have. In fact, it was the sweetest gift she'd ever received. And then there were their baths together. Oh, so much love and laughter. And the way Jace's eyes could turn all hot and fierce when he looked at her. The depths of passion he'd unlocked in her. So many things to recall. And all of them caused her to smile. And even to shed a tear or two. But they were tears of happiness. As she thought over this strange and wonderful weekend, she realized that what she and Jace had discovered was something rare and special. And maybe, just maybe, they could work things out so that they could still be together when their decisions were made.

It was true that she had a lot of things to sort out in her personal and professional life. The same was true for Jace. But if their feelings ran deep enough, and their concern for one another was sincere enough, they would find a way. After all, hadn't she overcome enormous obstacles on the way to achieving this career? What was to stop her from having it all? From having Jace in her life, as well as the career she wanted?

She would do it, she decided. They would do it. Together.

She found herself wondering about that little chapel Jace had mentioned. But she was too afraid to dwell on it. Jace had looked so surprised when he'd let that fact slip. And then he'd grown too quiet.

Regret, she thought. He regretted saying anything.

Still, she couldn't help hoping. And in some small corner of her mind, she was convinced that he wanted what she wanted.

Her spirits were so high that she found herself laughing with delight when she heard the sound of the Jeep. She raced across the room and threw open the door.

Jace climbed the steps. In his hands were two heaping grocery bags.

"With all that food, it looks like you're planning on spending a long time up here in your self-imposed isolation."

"Could be."

She held the door as he stepped inside and carried the bags to the kitchen counter.

"So." She watched as he deposited his burden. "How were the roads?"

"They're clear." With his back to her he began unloading the sacks.

"Did you look over that chapel?"

There was a moment of complete silence.

She felt suddenly awkward. That had definitely been the wrong thing to say. To fill the void she said, "You were gone so long I was beginning to think you weren't coming back." She laughed again, remembering Jace's little joke when she'd returned from her long walk up the mountain. "I figured you'd decided to keep right on going."

"I'll admit I thought about it. It was more than a little tempting."

It was the tone of his voice that made her smile

fade. And then, as he turned toward her, she caught sight of the angry look on his face. The silly, teasing words she'd been about to say died on her lips.

"Jace, what is it? What's wrong?"

"Wrong? How could anything be wrong?" His words were laced with sarcasm. "I guess I've just been out of the country too long. I haven't developed that keen sense of humor that's so prevalent in Hollywood these days."

"Sense of humor? I don't understand what brought this on—"

He tossed down a handful of newspapers and tabloids. "I told you I was a newsaholic. The first thing I reached for when I hit the store was a stack of newspapers. Imagine my surprise when I saw your face on every one of these."

Ciara snatched them up. Each of them showed photos of her under glaring headlines. One read Hollywood Star Missing From Own Marriage. Another, showing a photo of Ciara in a wedding gown, blared The Runaway Bride, and stated that the actress had left her fiancé practically at the altar. The tabloids were even worse, showing photo spreads of several pages long, with Ciara in various states of undress, followed by extensive interviews with Brendan Swift. In fact, Brendan seemed to be everywhere. Quoted on the news, on talk shows, on morning shows and late shows. He had, Ciara realized, used every opportunity to enhance his own publicity.

She read quickly, the words leaping out at her. In every interview, Brendan portrayed himself as the confused, brokenhearted lover who had absolutely no idea why she'd left so soon before the wedding. But he exhorted his friends in the press to aid in his search for his beloved bride-to-be, who would surely be returning soon, repentant and eager to make amends for having worried him and all her friends in this manner. He insisted that the wedding would take place next weekend as planned. And why wouldn't it? They were two people deeply in love.

Jace watched Ciara as she scanned the photos and related articles. "I don't hear you denying it. It's true then? You're engaged to Brendan Swift?"

She swallowed. Nodded. "Technically, I suppose—"

"The wedding is next weekend. And you just somehow forgot to mention it?" His eyes blazed.

"I didn't forget. I just—"

"You just thought you'd keep that little detail to yourself."

When she said nothing, he lowered his voice until it was a fierce whisper. "I take it he was one of those...things you came here to work out."

"Yes." The word stuck in her throat like a knife. "And I should have told you about him. It was wrong. But I didn't want to talk about him. Not when I...not when we..." She stopped, unable to go on.

"Not when we were having such a good time helping each other forget our troubles. Is that what you were going to say? Why muddy the waters with a fiancé? After all, the poor dumb fool will still be there, waiting for you when you come back. I took the time to read a couple of these...pieces of journalistic trash. He says in every interview that he still loves you. And you love him. And the wedding plans are still in place. As for me, hell, I must have come off like the biggest of fools. Ready, willing and able. Just look at you. You had the best of both worlds. A hotshot actor waiting at the altar, and a chance for one last fling with a sex-starved reporter. I guess that's the ultimate revenge, isn't it? Why spoil a good thing with the truth? Isn't that right, Hollywood?"

"That isn't fair, Jace. I—"

"Fair?" His hand closed around her upper arm, dragging her close. His eyes were hot with fury, burning into her with such intensity that she was forced to look away. "You're going to lecture me on what's fair?"

"No. I admit I was wrong. But I came here to think. To decide my future. Not just Brendan, but my career. I didn't come here expecting to meet someone who would mean—"

He flung her away from him, as though the touch of her burned him. He didn't want to hear anything more. Every word out of her mouth cut like a razor. "Go on, Hollywood. Run back to your Malibu beach house, and your career and your—understanding fiancé. I'm sure the two of you have played this little game often enough that it keeps your relationship interesting."

She rubbed her arm, and struggled to keep her tone reasonable. "Jace, listen to me a minute. This wasn't a game. I didn't plan this any more than you did. But it happened. And now that it has, I don't know how to make it right."

"I do. Oh, I know how to make it right. You can leave me alone. It's what I wanted when I first came here."

"But you haven't heard—"

"I've heard more than enough. All I want now is for you to leave." He turned away and began unloading the sacks of groceries, effectively shutting her out.

She stood a moment, swamped with emotions. How could she possibly explain what had happened here? What had seemed wonderful, beautiful, was suddenly sounding cheap and sordid. The very thought of it pushed her to the edge. She knew that if she didn't leave now, she would embarrass herself and burst into tears.

She picked up her bag, as she opened the door and turned for one last glimpse of Jace. He kept his back to her, refusing to even acknowledge her departure.

She walked out, and pulled the door shut behind her. As she descended the steps and made her way to the shed, she silently prayed he would relent and call her back, so that she could explain. Or try to.

Ciara got into the car; she turned the key, and the engine purred. As she backed out of the shed, she glanced toward the window of the cabin. Inside, she could see Jace, exactly where she'd left him. He didn't even turn as she maneuvered the car around his Jeep and started down the curving, tree-lined trail. Then she was out onto the highway.

Less than a mile from the cabin she passed the little chapel. It was, as Jace had described it, a small country church, with ivy climbing the stone walls, and sunlight reflecting off lovely stained-glass windows. It looked as though it had been there, gracing the landscape, forever.

Maybe it was the sight of the church. Or the image that flashed into her mind of Jace's quick smile as he'd spoken of it, hinting that it would make a lovely, romantic wedding chapel. Whatever the reason, Ciara felt herself go numb and was forced to pull off the road.

She sat, hunched over the wheel, staring at her hands—and seeing Jace's. Big and strong, holding her, comforting her, making her feel as if she'd come home. His strong fingers lacing with hers, leading her up a mountain to a place where the air was so clean it hurt the lungs. And now her lungs felt as though they would burst with the pain throbbing inside them. But she was afraid to allow the release of tears. If they started, they might never end.

She felt like an open wound, unable to stop bleeding. As though she had been peeled away from him, and bits and pieces of him were stuck to her. In her mind she could see his eyes, which had gazed on her with such tenderness, but which were now so hot and fierce that they pierced her very soul. She could hear his voice, once deep and rich and warm with laughter, now scorching her with cruel, sarcastic words.

The thought of his furious accusations drained away all her hard-won self-esteem. For she knew he'd spoken the truth. In the beginning she hadn't told him about Brendan because of her natural reticence with reporters. But later, she had concealed the truth because she hadn't wanted to spoil what had developed between them. Brendan had no place in this. He had ceased to matter to her at all. Now that she had tasted real passion, real caring and concern in Jace's arms, she knew she could never accept less. Not from Brendan. Not from anyone, ever again. If anyone had told her that she would find everything she'd ever wanted in a deserted mountain cabin, in the space of a single weekend, she would have scoffed. But it was true. She'd found it all. But that didn't excuse her behavior. Jace had every right to feel betrayed. And now, she must pay the price of that betrayal. She had to accept the fact that she had lost Jace's love and respect forever.

What had her mother always told her? *You can't make someone love you. All you can do is be someone deserving of love.* Right now she didn't feel very deserving of Jace's love. Of anyone's love. It was just one more thing she'd have to deal with.

Nearly an hour later she managed to pull herself together. Squaring her shoulders she turned on the engine and pulled out onto the main highway. A highway that led away from the peace and contentment she'd found with Jace. And back to all the troubles she'd left behind in California.

Jace lifted the ax, swung, and neatly split the log, sending the pieces flying in all directions. Without taking time to stack them, he positioned another log and did the same. Then another and another, until all around him the ground was littered. It seemed fitting somehow. A reminder of the debris that remained of his once-ordered life.

If he thought he'd suffered demons before coming here, they were nothing compared to those he was now facing. He needed the release of hard, physical work to dispel these new ones. Anger. Jealousy. Humiliation. With every stroke of the ax he cursed and called himself every kind of fool.

He'd once thought of himself as a fairly intelligent man. A man with clear-cut goals that he pursued with absolute intensity. But what he'd indulged in this weekend was madness. It had to be a form of madness, brought on by the bombing and the losses he'd experienced as a result. What else would explain why he pursued Ciara Wilde? Why he would build her up in his own mind until she became his obsession? He'd given in to every fantasy, practically ravishing her the first time he took her. And after that, he'd been insatiable. Had been unable to get enough of her.

Even now—knowing she'd been dishonest with him, knowing she'd deliberately misled him—he wanted her. And if she were to drive back up this lane, he'd have her out of that car and into his bed so fast her head would be spinning.

That made him the biggest fool of all.

He brought the ax down again, biting into the log with such force that he could feel every one of his muscles protest. But he couldn't stop. He worked until exhaustion had him dropping to the ground, where he sat, taking deep drafts and cursing his own traitorous heart.

The closer Ciara got to home, the more her recriminations faded and her temper rose. How dare Jace Lockhart accuse her of lying. She hadn't lied. Nor had she misled him. She had simply chosen not to tell him everything. Maybe it was wrong. But it wasn't done to be cruel, but rather to spare him, and herself.

What about Jace's intentions? Had they been any nobler? Hadn't he used her to ease his own pain? And though she'd tried to tell herself she meant something to him, he'd never spoken of a future together. A commitment. In fact, hadn't he told her that he'd needed no one, and nothing, except the next assignment, the next unknown country, the next challenge—?

She went perfectly still, catching her breath on the pain as the thought filled her mind. Even as denial washed over her, she couldn't completely dismiss the idea. For a man who'd lived his life on such a fast track, the sameness of days and nights in a cabin, with no power, no stimulation, would surely have become unbearable. Unless... She swallowed, forcing herself to consider the possibility.

Unless he created a new challenge.

What better challenge could there be for a dangerous, reckless man than to see just how far he could get with a famous actress? Especially one who had made it plain that she didn't trust reporters.

Oh, she'd made it so easy. She'd fallen willingly into his arms. Like some silly, lovesick fool.

Hadn't she learned anything after all these years? Hadn't she been exploited often enough? Hadn't she been used and abused by people who called themselves her friends? What had made her think Jace Lockhart would be any better than the rest?

True, he'd been a thoughtful, tender lover. And he'd gone out of his way to lift her spirits and her self-esteem. But maybe it was all an act. A clever act by a smooth operator who knew exactly how to get what he wanted.

Now he had the interview of a lifetime. He would be able to scoop all the other reporters who'd been scouring the countryside, in search of the big story. What a story he'd have to tell. And what a receptive audience he'd find in the tabloids.

By the time Ciara arrived at her home in Malibu, she felt a wave of bitter exhaustion. All this thinking had solved nothing. It had just made her even more confused, and more miserable. One minute she loved Jace, the next she hated him. And hated herself even more.

She caught sight of the news van seconds after she turned off the engine. Retrieving her bag from the back seat of her car, she raced for the safety of her door, only to find a cluster of reporters barring her way.

She dragged in a deep breath and prepared herself

for the assault. As microphones were thrust in her face and the glare of flashbulbs and bright lights blinded her, she pasted on her professional smile.

Her voice was the smooth, polished voice she'd used hundreds of times in movies and interviews. There was no hint of the accent that she had so determinedly erased over the years, with the help of voice coaches. Nor was there a trace of the fear that dogged her footsteps. If she wavered for a few moments, those who watched and listened thought it was only because she was pondering her answers.

In front of the world, her eyes remained dry. The bitter tears would come later, when she could afford the luxury of a moment of privacy. Then, and only then, would she indulge her battered, broken heart, and allow her grief to show.

Fifteen

Jace stayed at the cabin for a month after Ciara left. It had taken that long for him to lick his wounds and prepare to face civilization again. Now, as he swung his car through the arched entryway in the sandstone wall surrounding the Fortune ranch, he paused a moment to stare at the sweep of land that never failed to stir his heart. This land belonged to his childhood. A very large part of his childhood. And though he had no desire to live here again, he always enjoyed his visits. This was more than a visit, of course. It was a command performance. To celebrate the wedding of his nephew Logan Fortune to Emily Applegate.

He chafed at the stiff collar of the formal shirt. It had been at Mary Ellen's insistence that he wore a tux to her son's wedding—over his loud, and at times profane, protests. He brought his car to a stop at the long curving stone walkway and stepped out, tossing his keys to a young man hired to park their cars.

"Good afternoon, sir."

"'Afternoon. Just wait until I get my jacket." He opened the back door and lifted his tuxedo jacket from its hanger, then slipped it on as he took the adobe steps two at a time. He turned the handle of the antique wooden door and paused beneath the covered entryway.

"Jace." As soon as she spotted him coming through the doorway, Mary Ellen hurried over. She gave him a long, admiring glance. "I can't believe it. You're on time. And you wore your tuxedo."

"Only because you threatened murder and mayhem if I didn't."

"And it worked. You look handsome."

"I look like a penguin."

"Okay. A very handsome penguin." She tucked her arm through his. "Have you made a decision about your future?"

"More or less. I'm going to accept the offer to teach."

"And the book?"

He nodded. "Yeah. I've already started it."

"Oh, Jace. I just know it'll be wonderful."

He laughed, squeezed her arm. "Spoken like a devoted sister. At least I can always count on selling one copy."

"I'll buy hundreds. And give them to all my friends. Come on—" she glanced around "—before we start to mingle, there are a few things I'd better tell you."

"I promise, I won't eat with my fingers. And I won't bore anyone with war stories."

She playfully smacked his arm. "Stop teasing. This is important."

"Okay. What do you have to tell me?"

"Well, remember how I told you that Matthew and

Claudia's son Bryan had been kidnapped last summer. And then how the FBI had recovered a boy believed to be Bryan. But that child wasn't Bryan—in fact, no one knows who the boy's parents are. But they do know he's a Fortune because he has the hereditary crown-shaped birthmark and rare blood type. So all the Fortune men had to undergo DNA testing, to determine the father of little Taylor—that's what they're calling the mystery baby. And hopefully the results of the testing will also give the police some leads as to baby Bryan's whereabouts."

Jace frowned. "So, how soon will we know?"

"Soon, I hope. Claudia and Matthew are wonderful surrogate parents to Taylor, but everyone can tell that the stress of waiting and wondering about the fate of their son Bryan is wearing on their marriage. The tension is getting to everyone. I just wanted to warn you that tempers might flare."

"That won't be anything new, will it?"

His sister shook her head. "Not with this family. Come on. Let's mingle."

Jace plucked a glass of champagne from a passing waiter's tray, to fortify himself for the coming siege. Then he allowed his sister to lead him toward the other guests.

Ciara entered the Fortune home, confidence in her step and her head held high. At long last she knew who she was and where she was headed. She was feeling better about herself than she could ever have believed possible. And it showed. In her walk—easy, purposeful. In her smile, which lit up her face and added a sparkle to her eyes. In her whole demeanor. It no longer mattered if people stared and pointed, or stopped what they were doing to whisper as she passed by. She'd put her distasteful past behind her, and was actually looking forward to the future for the first time in years.

"Ciara." Eden crossed the room and kissed her. Then she caught both Ciara's hands and held her a little away, studying the way she looked in the long column of pale lemon silk. It had a high, mandarin collar with a row of frog closings that ran from her shoulder to her hip, and a slender, slitted skirt that ended at her ankles. "I don't think I've ever seen you look so beautiful."

"I might say the same about you. You're positively glowing, Eden."

"Thank you." Eden turned to include the couple who stood beside her. "Ciara Wilde, I'd like you to meet my brother Holden Fortune, his wife Lucy, and their new baby, April."

"A new baby? Congratulations. Oh, just look at her."

Lucy proudly lifted the lace shawl to reveal her infant daughter, while Holden stood beside his wife, beaming with pride.

"She's just beautiful. I'm so envious." Ciara glanced around. "Eden, where's your son Sawyer? I've been dying to meet him."

"Over there." Eden pointed and waved the little

boy over. "Sawyer, I'd like you to meet my friend Miss Wilde. Remember I told you about her?"

The five-year-old presented his hand to shake Ciara's. "Hello, Sawyer. It's very nice to meet such a polite young man. And one so big and handsome."

He gave her a big grin. "That's what everybody says when they see me."

"That's because it's true. I bet you'll grow to be over six feet tall."

"Really? That big?"

"Uh-huh. I just hope the next time I see you, you're not bigger than me."

"If I am," he said, suddenly shy, "can I still hug you?"

"You'd better. Or you'll make me sad. I expect you to give me hugs even when you're a grown-up man and I'm an old lady."

"My mom says you're never going to look old, 'cause you're just too pretty." All shyness and formality gone, he hugged her and Ciara closed her eyes a moment, loving the way he felt in her arms. If she could have one more blessing in her life, it would be this: a sweet, unspoiled child, who would give her wet, sticky kisses and warm, loving hugs.

He looked at her for a silent moment. Then, as children do, his attention shifted. He said, "Come on, Mama. You promised me a glass of soda."

"So I did." She turned to Ciara with a smile. "I'll see you in a few minutes."

Ciara nodded and watched as mother and son walked away. She'd only known Eden a few months—Emily had introduced them. Yet, she felt as though they'd been friends forever. Eden was so warm and friendly, a person couldn't help but like her instantly. But Ciara had sensed a hidden sadness behind her eyes the first time they'd met. Ciara knew what that kind of pain was like and had immediately felt a sisterly bond with Eden.

Across the room she caught a glimpse of broad shoulders in an elegantly tailored tuxedo. Though the man was surrounded by a cluster of people, and his back was to her, she knew immediately who he was. Her throat went dry. She had known, of course, that Jace would be here. Emily and Eden had both told her the names of the guests. Though nerves fluttered in the pit of her stomach, she took a deep calming breath. She was certain she could get through this.

She had barely taken two steps before she heard her name called out. She turned to see her best friend from childhood, Emily Applegate, hiding behind a half-opened door. She hurried over and was quickly hauled inside. The door was swiftly and firmly closed behind her.

"Oh, Emily. Just look at you." Ciara felt tears sting her eyes as the bride-to-be twirled to show off her gown. "I've never seen a more beautiful bride."

Emily hugged her and wiped a tear of her own. "I'm so glad we've remained close friends over the years and that you're here to share this day with me. We both sure have come a long way from Kentucky."

"That's the truth! You know I wouldn't have missed your wedding for anything." Then, careful not to wrinkle the bride's gown, she gave her a hug. "Are you nervous?"

"A little. But I know the nerves will all be behind me when I look into Logan's eyes."

Ciara felt more tears threaten. "It's just wonderful to see the two of you finally discovering true love. Of course, we all knew it before either of you did. I could tell when we had lunch in San Antonio a few months ago that he was special to you."

"I guess that's true of most couples. We often can't see what's right there in front of our eyes. But we're all so afraid of being hurt." She touched a hand to Ciara's. "Are you all right?"

"I'm fine." She smiled and leaned close for another quick hug. "Really. I'll see you soon. After you've become Mrs. Logan Fortune."

"Doesn't that have a nice ring to it?"

"It does. I'm so happy for you, Emily."

Ciara slipped out of the room and made her way toward the library, hoping for a moment to compose herself. As she stepped inside she realized she wasn't alone. A couple stood across the room, their heads bent in quiet conversation. She recognized Ryan Fortune and Lily Cassidy. She'd met them once a few months ago when visiting Eden. Before she could slip away, she heard "You know I love you, Lily."

"I know. Is that why you brought me in here? Just to tell me that?"

"No. Yes." Ryan's tone was rough with frustration. "I don't like seeing you hurt. You know I want to marry you, Lily. But this divorce, and the kidnapping, are taking their toll. I just don't want you to lose patience with me."

Lily lifted a hand to stroke his cheek. "I'm never going to lose patience with you, Ryan. I'll wait for you for as long as it takes. Haven't I proved as much these past thirty-five years?"

His hands closed over her shoulders. "Oh, Lily. This is why I love you so. God knows, I don't deserve you."

When the two embraced, Ciara turned away and hurried down the hall, embarrassed that she'd eavesdropped on such an intimate scene. But the image of the two lovers was imprinted on her mind. It added another layer of pain around her heart. Everyone, it seemed, had someone to love. Everyone except...

When she returned to the living room she was quickly drawn into a circle of acquaintances who were eager to welcome her to the Fortune ranch.

"Ciara," Eden called, "have you met Savannah and Cruz Perez? Cruz recently started up his own horse-breeding operation at a ranch near here."

"That's wonderful." Ciara smiled in greeting, then, spying the bundle in Savannah's arms said, "And who is this?"

"This is our son, Dylan." Savannah turned so that the infant, pressed to her shoulder, could be admired.

"Oh, he's adorable." Ciara struggled to ignore the yearning. *All things in their own good time,* her mother used to say. It just wasn't her time yet. But when would her time come?

She opened her arms. "Would you mind if I held him for a moment?"

Savannah and Cruz exchanged smiles. Then Savannah handed him over, and watched admiringly as Ciara pressed her lips to his soft little cheek.

"Oh, there's just something about the smell of a baby. He's absolutely perfect. You're so blessed."

Savannah and Cruz glanced at each other over her head. The look they gave said, more than any words, that they were well aware of their blessings.

At the sight of Ciara, Jace went perfectly still. He'd known she would be here. He'd wheedled the guest list out of his sister. But nothing could have prepared him for this first glimpse of her.

She wore her hair soft and loose, just the way he loved it. The dress was surprisingly simple. Not at all like the gowns she wore in her movies. This one was high-necked and fluid, skimming her body without being revealing. She managed to look demure and sexy at the same time. Cool and elegant. And completely untouchable.

His hand tightened on the stem of his glass as he thought of the body beneath that dress. A body he had come to know intimately. Though the voices continued around him, he didn't hear a word. He was so intent upon watching her, he didn't even notice when his sister directed a question to him.

"...isn't that right, Jace?"

"Hmm?" He turned his head, forced a smile. "Yes. Of course."

He caught sight of Ciara cradling Savannah's baby in her arms and felt something pierce his heart. He turned away, only to see Claudia and Matthew approaching, their faces showing the strain of the kidnapping.

Jace pressed a kiss to Claudia's cheek and shook Matthew's hand. "I'm sorry that there's been no news."

The two of them exchanged a glance before Matthew managed to say, "Thank heaven for Taylor. Most of the time he keeps us too busy to think."

At the mention of the boy they'd temporarily adopted while waiting for news of their son Bryan, Jace noticed that several in their party became a little too quiet. The uneasiness over the DNA test results had all the Fortunes on edge.

He looked up to see Eden link her arm through Ciara's and start leading her toward their group. The two women had their heads close together, whispering, and the sound of Ciara's laughter was so sweet that Jace found himself draining his glass and reaching for another.

Ryan and Lily stopped the two women, and they paused halfway across the room. At a question, Ciara removed a photograph from her small, jeweled handbag, and passed it around.

"Quite the heartbreaker," he heard Eden remark. "Oh, Ciara. You're so lucky."

"I know. I just love him."

Jace's heart plummeted. What had he expected? That she would somehow put her life on hold and wait for him to make another move? Not a smart woman like Ciara. He glanced around, looking for an escape.

"Ciara." Eden was smiling as she led her friend forward. "I think you know everyone here, don't you?"

"Yes." Ciara offered her cheek to Mary Ellen and shook hands with Claudia and Matthew. Ryan and Lily joined them, as did Lucy and Holden, who was now cuddling his baby, April, to his heart.

"Have you met Jace Lockhart?"

"Yes. We've met." She hadn't told anyone—not even Emily or Eden—about their snowbound encounter. Ciara inclined her head. "Hello, Jace."

He realized that she was holding back, reluctant to touch him. Something perverse in his nature made him offer his hand, knowing there was no gracious way she could refuse. "Ciara. How are you?"

Her head came up—just a fraction. And her eyes widened. Then she placed her hand in his.

She'd prepared for this meeting as she would have prepared for any role. Had gone over what she would say, and how she would act in his presence. But that had been role-playing. This was reality. She could actually feel the pulse of heat between them when their hands touched. And could see the challenge in his eyes when he looked at her. She withdrew her hand quickly, and lowered it to her side. But she could still feel the tingling in her fingertips, like an electrical charge. Damn him for having this effect on her.

"Congratulations, Ciara." Ryan touched a hand to her shoulder. "Eden says you've sold your first screenplay."

"Yes." Her eyes softened. This was something she was comfortable talking about. "Production starts in the fall. We're hoping Elise Crompton will agree to direct."

"Elise Crompton?" Mary Ellen frowned. "Didn't she just win an award for her last film?"

Ciara nodded. "She's really well-respected in the industry. She's crazy about this script."

"Does this mean you're giving up acting?" Mary Ellen asked.

"Not altogether. But I'll be a lot more careful about what roles I'll accept in the future. For now, I want to concentrate on my writing."

Mary Ellen glanced toward her brother. "You and Jace would probably find a lot to talk about, since he's writing a book."

"A...book?" Ciara looked at him and found him staring at her with such intensity that she had to avoid his eyes.

"Maybe he'll tell you about it." Mary Ellen laughed. "He won't say a word to anyone else about it. I don't know what it's about or even where it's supposed to take place."

"Probably one of those far-flung exotic places he's been to." Ryan gave Jace an admiring glance. "You've got the perfect background for a writer, Jace. A television reporter who's been everywhere. If you were selling stock in yourself, I'd buy all the shares allowed. I have a feeling you're going to become so successful you'll probably be a household name in the next few years.''

"I will if my sister has anything to say about it. She's offered to buy up all the copies and give them to her friends. It may be the only way my publisher will be able to get it off the shelves.''

"So, you already have a publisher?" Ryan shook his head. "I'm impressed. I hope you'll let me know when it's coming out.''

"Don't worry,'' Mary Ellen said with a laugh. "Knowing my reclusive brother, he won't say a word. But I'll tell the whole world.''

Jace pressed a kiss to his sister's cheek. "You've always done enough talking for the both of us.'' He glanced around, careful not to look at Ciara. "If you'll excuse me.'' Without explaining where he was going, he walked away.

Ciara expelled the long, deep breath she hadn't even known she was holding. She'd been afraid to move. She couldn't recall a single word she'd spoken. And all because of Jace Lockhart.

It certainly hadn't taken him long to escape. It was obvious he didn't want to be anywhere near her.

She needed some air. Seeing Sawyer out on the patio, she seized the opportunity. She squeezed Eden's hand and whispered, "There's a certain handsome young man out there I'd like to spend some time getting to know.''

Eden followed her glance and, seeing her son, laughed. "I told him if he spilled a single drop of that soda, he'd lose it. I guess he isn't taking any chances.''

''Smart boy. I'm going to join him.''

She stepped out into the warm sunshine and paused to watch as Sawyer chased after a butterfly. When it lifted high in the air, he returned his attention to the glass of soda.

''Are you having a good time?'' Ciara asked.

He nodded. ''I was hoping to catch that butterfly. But it got away.''

She knelt down beside him. ''They have a way of doing that. It's just as well. Their wings are so delicate, they can be broken if you just squeeze your hands together too tightly.''

''I wouldn't hurt it.''

''I know you wouldn't want to. But it can happen by accident. Sometimes, when we hold on too tightly, we hurt the very things we love. And you wouldn't want to break those pretty wings, would you?''

''Uh-uh.'' He looked up so trustingly into her eyes that Ciara felt her heart ache. ''I just wanted to hold it. Like a pet.''

''I understand. Speaking of pets...'' She reached into her handbag and pulled out the photograph. ''Did you see mine?''

His eyes widened. ''He's yours? What's his name?''

''Blizzard.''

''Wow. I wish my mom would get me a puppy.''

''I bet she will when you get a little older. They're a lot of work, and you'll have to prove to your mom that you're willing to clean up all the messes that are bound to happen with a puppy.''

"Has Blizzard made messes?"

She nodded. "Lots of them."

"Do you get mad at him?"

"How can I get mad? He's just a baby."

"Will you bring him over for me to play with sometime?"

"I will. I promise."

He glanced toward the door, then said, "I'd better go inside. Want to come with me?"

She shook her head. "I think I'll just wait out here awhile."

"Okay. Bye." He hugged her, then danced away.

She stood, smoothing down her skirt. As she turned, she caught sight of Jace leaning against the wall, smoke from his cigar curling over his head.

She brought her hand to her throat in a gesture of surprise. "I didn't realize you were there."

"Yeah. I could tell." She'd been so relaxed and easy with Sawyer. It had been a joy to watch her. Joy, mingled with sorrow. If only she could be that easy and relaxed with him. But he'd managed to ruin whatever chance he'd had.

Ciara studied the way he looked, leaning comfortably against the wall, ankles crossed. Yet the relaxed pose seemed a contradiction. She could sense a tension in him. In the way he looked at her. In the hand, clenched at his side.

He still had the ability to hurt her, she realized. Just

seeing him here caused a pain inside her that couldn't be denied.

A maid came by with a tray of hors d'oeuvres. Ciara shook her head. The thought of food made her stomach clench.

When the maid walked away, Jace kept his tone even. "Congratulations on the screenplay. I know it means a lot to you." She smelled the way he remembered. Soap-and-water clean. At the thought of burying his face in her hair and breathing her in until he was drunk with her, a little muscle began working in his jaw.

"Thanks. I'm really excited about it. Congratulations on your book as well. Have you already started it?"

"I have the first couple of chapters roughed in. It helps that I had deadlines to meet for so many years. I'm trying to keep that same discipline and focus now."

"I'm not surprised. You're a disciplined man, Jace." And so handsome, she thought. There was just something about a man in a tuxedo. Especially when he was tall and rugged, with just a hint of danger. Oh, why did he have to look so good?

He cleared his throat, struggled to keep his tone even. "I have a lot more respect for what you're doing, now that I'm doing the same thing. The fact that you wrote your first screenplay while you were busy acting in films makes it even more amazing."

She flushed under his praise. Her heart felt as if it

had grown two sizes too big. "So when do you return to Europe?"

"I'm not going back."

She hoped her expression hadn't changed. "You mean you're staying here? In Texas?"

"No. I accepted a teaching job at a university. In California."

Her heartbeat sped up, and she had to pause a moment to catch her breath. "What part?"

"Southern California."

"I guess that means we'll be neighbors. Have you found a place to live?"

"Not yet. But I'm going to keep an eye out for something on the ocean. Malibu, maybe. I think...I'd like to watch the storms."

Was that laughter lurking in his eyes? She couldn't be certain without staring. And she was afraid to stare too deeply, for fear of what he'd see in her eyes. A hunger, a longing for what might have been.

"Maybe you'd like to look over my place. I'm thinking of selling it." She struggled to keep her tone casual.

"Why?"

"It's too big for one person."

"Just one?"

"Well, one person and a puppy."

He allowed himself to smile now, and his tone lightened. "I heard you telling Sawyer about your dog. Very interesting name." He wouldn't bother to tell her how relieved he'd been to learn that the photo wasn't of his competitor. "What breed?"

"Nothing fancy. I went to the dog pound." She laughed, and the sound of it washed over him, warming him. She pulled the photo from her purse. "Blizzard is just a mutt. A white, fuzzy little mutt, with overgrown paws and floppy ears, and the sweetest disposition in the world." She held the picture up for Jace's inspection. "I just love him. And best of all, he loves me."

"I don't blame him. A guy would have to be a fool not to."

"You mean 'a dog.'"

He blinked. "Isn't that what I said?"

"No. You said—"

"I know what I said." He debated for one more moment, then, tired of this verbal sparring, he put out his cigar and took her arm.

"Jace, what are you doing?"

"I just want to get away from these glass doors, and all those eyes watching us." He hauled her around the corner of the house.

"Whatever for?"

"No reason. I just prefer a little privacy."

"But the wedding's about to start any minute now."

"This won't take long. I want you to know that the quarter-of-a-million-dollar offer you warned me about actually happened."

"What are you talking about?"

"That first night at the cabin, you warned me that I'd have a hard time passing up a fortune to write about my weekend with Ciara Wilde."

"Somebody found out about us?"

He nodded, watching her eyes. "A very enterprising reporter showed up on my doorstep. It was only hours after you'd left. His magazine offered me a windfall to give them the details. But you were wrong about how hard it would be to refuse. As I recall, in my current mood that day, I nearly tore him limb from limb before he managed to escape to his car and drive away as fast as he could. I'm sure he's still telling everyone he meets about the madman he came upon at that cabin."

She smiled, remembering Jace's temper. "Poor guy. That's not the reception he'd expect to receive after offering all that money."

"No." His eyes narrowed slightly. "I read about your ex-fiancé. Are you hurt that he tied the knot only two weeks after you dumped him?"

"That's none of your business."

"Answer me. Are you hurt?"

"Why would I be?"

His eyes darkened. "Humor me, Hollywood. I need to know."

Hollywood. She nearly wept at his use of that name. "All right. If you must know, I was relieved. His new love interest attracted the media circus away from me. And since she loves the spotlight almost as much as Brendan does, I figure they'll be a perfect match. They'll both try to get all the publicity they can out of this marriage before it ends in a spectacular display of fireworks."

"It could have been you."

She nodded. "I guess I'm just unlucky in love."

"Yeah. Me too." He shot her that heart-stopping grin, and she felt her heart spinning dangerously out of control.

He touched a hand to her shoulder. When she didn't pull away, he leaned close. "I owe you an apology. I reacted to those tabloid headlines with all the finesse of a wounded grizzly."

"You were a bit rough." She could feel the heat of his touch through her clothes. When he leaned closer, the warmth of his breath whispered over her cheek, and she had to close her eyes for a moment to keep from pulling him to her. "But I deserved it. I had no right to keep my engagement a secret."

"Some secret. By the time I left the cabin I'd learned that everyone in this country knew about it. You couldn't help it if I was like an alien from another planet."

"Jace—"

He held up a hand. "I'm apologizing. Are you in a mood to accept that?"

She shrugged. "I guess...I'm apologizing, too."

"Accepted. Now to the really important thing."

She lifted her head. "What?"

"I heard what you told Sawyer. About not holding a butterfly too tightly, or you'll hurt it. You're like that to me—a beautiful butterfly. And I'm afraid I'll hurt you. But—" His hands were already on her shoulders, drawing her against him.

"Jace—"

"Shut up, Hollywood. I promise I won't hold you

so tight that I break your pretty wings. But I need to kiss you. Right now.''

His face lowered slowly to hers. So slowly that she felt her heart stop, and her throat close, just waiting. And then his lips were on hers, and everything she'd ever felt for him came spiraling upward, making her head whirl, and her heart tumble, until she had to grab on to him to keep from falling.

Against her lips he muttered, ''I've never known such happiness, or such misery, in my entire life. And it's all because of you. I realized, too late, that I love you, Ciara Wilde.''

''You…love me?'' She pushed away. Her eyes were wide, disbelieving.

''It must be love. Because all I can think of is spending the rest of my life with you. And Blizzard. And, hell…maybe a couple of kids, too.''

''Children? Jace, you…you want children?''

''I was looking around in there at all those happy parents, and it made me realize something. I've been chasing all over the world, and missing the most important things of all. I'd like a little girl first, with golden hair and laughing green eyes. And then, who knows? Maybe a half dozen of them after I get used to the idea.''

Her eyes filled and she blinked furiously.

''Hey.'' He lifted her face for his inspection. ''Tears, Hollywood?''

''Oh, Jace. I thought—I thought it was too late for us. I figured you could never forgive me for the mess I made.''

"*We* made." He brushed his lips over hers and felt his need for her rising. "And we'll probably make a few more. But as long as we make them together, we can clean them up. I never thought I'd hear myself say these words, but I want it all with you. I want to settle down. I want commitment, marriage and all that goes with it. Deal, Hollywood?"

She swallowed the lump that threatened to choke her. "Deal."

In the other room they could hear the music starting, signaling the beginning of the service.

Jace pressed his mouth to the hair at her temple and breathed her in, filling himself with the clean, fresh scent of her. "As soon as this is over, I'll race you to the cabin."

"Tonight?"

"I don't think I could wait another night. Say 'yes,' Hollywood."

She drew back and stared into his eyes, seeing a look of such hunger that her heart did another free fall. But she took a deep breath, determined to bargain. "I'll consider it. What does the winner get?"

"A wedding. In that little chapel near the cabin." He saw her eyes mist again.

"And the loser?"

He grinned, dragged her close. "A wedding. In that little chapel near the cabin."

"Covering all your bets, aren't you, Jace?"

"You bet, Hollywood. I learned from the expert. This time, win or lose, I have no intention of letting you get away. What do you say?"

She had no need for words. With all her feelings right there in her eyes for him to read, she wrapped her arms around his neck and offered her lips. Her kiss spoke of a passion so deep, they were both rocked by it. And of trust that this time, they would make it work. And of love. So much love.

Not the stuff of movies or novels. The real thing. Enough love to last for a lifetime and beyond.

* * * * *

Here's a preview of next month's

An aristocratic Fortune beauty is shocked to come face-to-face with her long-lost exotic lover.
Will she share her most sacred secret with the handsome sheikh—that he has a son?

THE SHEIKH'S SECRET SON
by
Kasey Michaels

He doesn't know, he doesn't know. And what he doesn't know can't hurt me.

Drawing on every resource at her command, her upbringing, her independent nature, her long years of taking care of herself, Eden Fortune willed her heart to slow. Willed her lips to smile. Willed herself to remember who she was, where she was and why she was here.

"You are looking well, Eden," Sheikh Ramir said, touching a hand to the soft, snow-white material that made up his headdress. He should have looked silly, or pretentious, dressed in his gray Armani suit, the headpiece held in place by two coils of something that looked very much like gold-wrapped silk, the edges of the material flowing over his shoulders.

But he didn't look silly. He looked wonderful. Dark, and mysterious, and somehow larger than life. Peter O'Toole as Lawrence of Arabia, but photographed in sepia tones. His eyes as dark as an Arabian night. His features chiseled from desert rock, weathered by desert winds. His tall form muscular but not muscle-bound. His movements measured, graceful.

His hands...well, she already knew about his hands.

"And you. You're…um…you're looking well,"
she answered at last, then cleared her throat. Maybe
the action would help her to breathe. But she doubted
it. "You knew I'd be here today?"

"Yes, Eden, I did. A knowledge you obviously did
not share."

Eden's temper hit her then, like a sharp slap on the
back meant to dislodge a bit of stuck fish bone—or
pride. "You're right, Your Highness. I had no knowledge that you'd be here today. That *Ben Ramsey*
would be here today."

He bowed slightly from the waist. It was a regal
inclination, and certainly no gesture that her words
had any impact on him, no sign of any reaction that
had even a nodding acquaintance with the word *embarrassed.*

She longed to clobber him with something hard and
heavy.

And then he really blew her mind…

"Very well," he said coldly. "If you wish to play
the innocent, Eden, I suppose I am willing to listen
as you tangle your tongue in knots, trying to deny yet
again that you knew who I was, who I am. Or is your
memory truly that faulty, that you forgot my letters,
my explanations? That you forgot to answer those
letters, just as you chose to forget me, forget Paris?"

"Letters? What letters? The only letter I ever received from you was the note you left on the bed.
Let's see, I think I still remember it. 'Eden, darling.
I have been called home. Stay where you are, I shall
contact you.' You signed it 'with love,' as I recall.''

She knew very well how he had signed the note, because she had kept it, for all these years. It was all she could ever give her son Sawyer of his father.

The anger was back, cold and hard. "Did I know you were really a sheikh, Ben? How was I supposed to know that? By reading between the lines of the note?"

When he said nothing, she stepped away from the table, picking up her attaché case as she headed past him toward the door. Then she turned. "I waited, Ben. I waited for nearly two weeks, long past the time I'd planned to return home, nearly too late to begin my next law-school term. I waited, and I worried, and I finally realized that I knew nothing about you. Nothing important—like where you lived, if you had a family. If you had a wife. Finally, I woke up, realized I'd just had myself a Paris fling, and chalked you up to experience. And that's how I'd like to keep it, Ben. An experience in my past, one I'm in no mood to repeat."

He took hold of her elbow—lightly, not really holding her in place, although she couldn't move. She was too shocked by the sensation his slight touch set off in her body, a warmth spreading throughout her, betraying her.

Eden chewed on the inside of her cheek, longing to tell him to go to hell. This fickle, duplicitous man she'd known as Ben Ramsey...the man whose child she'd secretly borne. A boy child, with his same aristocratic features, his same dark eyes and hair, his same elegant posture, his same almost princely air of confidence.

He doesn't know, she told herself, repeating the words over and over like a mantra. *He doesn't know.*

MONTANA MAVERICKS
Big Sky Brides

Legendary love comes to Whitehorn, Montana,
once more as beloved authors

Christine Rimmer, Jennifer Greene and Cheryl St.John

present three brand-new stories in this exciting anthology!

Meet the Brennan women:
SUZANNA, DIANA and ISABELLE

Strong-willed beauties who find unexpected
love in these irresistible marriage of
covnenience stories.

Don't miss
MONTANA MAVERICKS: BIG SKY BRIDES
On sale in February 2000,
only from Silhouette Books!

Available at your favorite retail outlet.

Celebrate Silhouette's 20th Anniversary

With beloved authors, exciting new miniseries and special keepsake collections, plus the chance to enter our 20th anniversary contest, in which one lucky reader wins the trip of a lifetime!

Take a look at who's celebrating with us:

DIANA PALMER

April 2000: SOLDIERS OF FORTUNE
May 2000 in Silhouette Romance: *Mercenary's Woman*

NORA ROBERTS

May 2000: IRISH HEARTS, the 2-in-1 keepsake collection
June 2000 in Special Edition: *Irish Rebel*

LINDA HOWARD

July 2000: MACKENZIE'S MISSION
August 2000 in Intimate Moments: *A Game of Chance*

ANNETTE BROADRICK

October 2000: a special keepsake collection,
plus a brand-new title in
November 2000 in Desire

Available at your favorite retail outlet.

Silhouette®

Where love comes alive™

Visit us at www.romance.net

PS20GEN